THE AMISH COWBOY'S JOURNEY

AMISH COWBOYS OF MONTANA
BOOK XI

ADINA SENFT

Copyright 2026 Shelley Adina Senft Bates

No part of this publication may be reproduced, distributed or transmitted in any form or by any means, including photocopying, recording, or other electronic or mechanical methods, without the prior written permission of the publisher, except in the case of brief quotations embodied in critical reviews and certain other noncommercial uses permitted by copyright law. For permission requests, write to the publisher at www.moonshellbooks.com.

This is a work of fiction. Names, characters, places, and incidents are a product of the author's imagination. Locales and public names are sometimes used for atmospheric purposes. Any resemblance to actual people, living or dead, or to businesses, companies, events, institutions, or locales is completely coincidental.

Cover design by Carpe Librum Book Design. Images used under license. "Great is Thy Faithfulness" by Thomas O. Chisholm, 1923, now in the public domain. Quotations from the King James Version of the Bible.

The Amish Cowboy's Journey / Adina Senft—1st ed.

ISBN 978-1-963929-84-3 R022426

 Formatted with Vellum

PRAISE FOR ADINA SENFT

"Adina Senft writes books that feel like drinking a warm cup of tea with a brown hen settled on your lap. I'll keep reading whatever she writes."

— REBECCA, GOODREADS, ON *THE AMISH COWBOY'S HOME*

"The first thing I loved about this story is that it's set in Montana, so it was fun to shift gears from farming to ranching. The Montana landscape in winter is an added bonus! I also loved that this is a prequel to Senft's Montana Millers series, the origin story, if you will, of the Circle M Ranch. This story is a girl-next-door romance with layered characters and an overall sweetness to the tone that warms the heart."

— READING IS MY SUPERPOWER, ON *THE AMISH COWBOY'S CHRISTMAS*

"As with all this series, *The Amish Cowboy's Mistake* was fantastic. Adina Senft has a way of composing a storyline that not only holds your attention, but leaves you with a better outlook on your own faith, family, and overall perspective."

— CHERESE A., GOODREADS, ON *THE AMISH COWBOY'S MISTAKE*

"Any book that can both entertain and leave me thinking is a book worth reading! Adina Senft is quickly becoming one of my favorite writers of Amish fiction.... Senft's characters are beautifully developed, [and] will move you to both laugh and cry."

— CHRISTIAN FICTION ADDICTION

IN THIS SERIES
AMISH COWBOYS OF MONTANA

The Amish Cowboy's Christmas prequel novella
The Amish Cowboy
The Amish Cowboy's Baby
The Amish Cowboy's Bride
The Amish Cowboy's Letter
The Amish Cowboy's Makeover
The Amish Cowboy's Home
The Amish Cowboy's Refuge
The Amish Cowboy's Mistake
The Amish Cowboy's Little Matchmakers
The Amish Cowboy's Wedding Quilt
The Amish Cowboy's Journey

Rose's July Surprise (book 7, Amish Romance Birthdays series)

CAST OF CHARACTERS
THE AMISH COWBOY'S JOURNEY

The Stolzfus family

- Rose Stolzfus, widow, owner of Rose Garden Quilts
- Alden Stolzfus, blacksmith/farrier, and Malena Miller (engaged to be married January 12)
- Julie Stolzfus
- Beth Stolzfus

The Millers at the Wild Rose Amish Inn

- Rachel Miller and Luke Hertzler (engaged to be married October 4)
- Tobias Miller, father of twins Gracie and Benny, married Sylvia Keim (28) on August 30
- Gideon Miller and special friend Patricia King
- Susanna Miller and Stephen Kurtz (engaged to be married October 11)
- Seth Miller

In the van

- Lori Turnbull, *Englisch* driver
- Chris and Jeannie Kauffman, Whinburg Township, PA, chaperones
- Jeannie's sister Delia Wagler, Whinburg Township, PA
- Chris's brothers Peter and Jude Kauffman, Whinburg Township, PA
- Catherine Yutzy and brother Carl, Amity, CO
- Emily Kuepfer and Janelle Stutzman, Prince Edward Island
- Tim Eicher, Beth Stolzfus, and Seth Miller, Mountain Home, MT

THE AMISH COWBOY'S JOURNEY

MOUNTAIN HOME, MONTANA

August 30
Tobias Miller and Sylvia Keim's wedding day

STANDING at the top of the stairs in the Keim farmhouse, Seth Miller's older brother Gideon grinned at the list of names in his hand. Then he lifted his gaze to Seth in that particular way that had always made Seth's heart sink. Gid had had exactly that mischief in his eyes when he'd egged Seth on at the top of the diving cliff. When he'd told him that skiing was fun. And now, as part of his duties as the elder of Tobias's *Neuwesitzern*, he was about to call out the name of Seth's supper partner.

Sharon Keim. Come on, Gid. Do me a favor. We're both our brother's supporters. We have a little extra grace today. Sylvia has to have picked Sharon Keim for me.

"Seth Miller and Beth Stolzfus!"

Disappointment landed in his stomach with a thud and he shot Gideon a scathing glare as Beth came out of the bedroom where the girls were waiting. He had enough manners to wipe it off his face, though, as Beth reached him and held out her hand. He took it with all the grace he could muster and together they walked down the stairs to take their places at the supper tables with the other couples his new sister-in-law Sylvia had paired up.

Gideon, of course, would go down the stairs last with Patricia King. Those two weren't talking wedding favors and china patterns yet, of course, but in Seth's mind, it was only a matter of time.

"Calvin Yoder and Clara King."

The strangest pairing ever, but rumor had it that Clara had whispered her wish to be Calvin's partner to the bride-to-be last church Sunday. And Sylvia, being the kindest person on the planet, had made it happen. Obviously Seth should have spoken to her personally instead of depending on his skunk of a brother.

His sister Susanna and her intended, Stephen Kurtz. Of course. They were getting married the week after their mother Rachel married Luke Hertzler, before the autumn Communion.

"Sharon Keim and Tim Eicher."

What was Sylvia thinking? Tim was way too old for Sharon. And of course they chose the seats next to him and Beth. Now he had to put a *gut* face on it and try to make conversation with silent Beth while not paying too much attention to bubbly, pretty, popular Sharon.

"Ruthanne Eicher and David Yoder."

Sharon and Beth stifled simultaneous moans of sympathy for poor Ruthanne. She must be the last of the *Youngie* not to have been asked for a date by "D for Desperate," as Susanna called the poor guy. Seth was no catch himself, but even he was tempted to take Dave aside and give him some advice. *Stop chasing everything in skirts.* That would be the first thing. *Don't be such a stick in the mud with all your rules and expectations.* That would be the second. *Nobody wants to feel like they're not good enough for you when they're more than you deserve.*

"I'd say *better her than me*, but that would be mean," Beth said.

For a moment, Seth though someone else must have spoken. Beth hardly ever did. He'd actually wondered if there was something wrong with her—she could go an entire day among the *Gmay*, like today, and not speak.

"Has he asked you out?" Sharon wanted to know. "He's asked me something like four times. Finally Onkel Josiah had to speak to him to make him stop."

"*Ja*. He and Calvin were helping with the renovations at our place, and he grabbed the first opportunity to ask both Julie and me, one after the other."

"Did you go out with him?" Seth blurted. But she couldn't have. Everyone would know if she had.

Beth lifted her chin. "None of your business. But Julie said no flat out."

Sharon laughed, a sound as delightful and sparkly as a creek after spring breakup. Hearing it made up a little for being snubbed. "He must have been crazy to ask your sister," Sharon said. "Unless he offered to take her to a hockey game."

Beth shook her head sadly. "No hockey in July, so he was out of luck both ways."

Seth had recovered from the snub now. "You're the perfect woman for him."

"Why do you say that?" Tim Eicher asked incredulously. He'd known Dave Yoder all his life.

"Because Dave's dream is to marry a woman who won't talk back. Beth hardly talks at all." He grinned at her, daring her to prove him wrong.

"Don't be silly, Seth," Sharon chided him, half laughing. "Beth talks. Just like she is now."

But as if to prove him right, that was the last time he heard her voice during the whole dinner. Not even Sharon could get her to say a thing, which in the end turned out to be a plus— he got to talk to Sharon, even if he had to share her attention with Tim. When Tobias and Sylvia came to their table to give each of them a piece of wedding cake wrapped in a paper doily and tied with ribbons in their wedding colors, Beth only smiled in thanks.

She had to join in the singing after dinner. It was unheard of not to sing at an Amish wedding.

So when he heard her clear voice taking the alto part for a rather daring four-part rendition of "Walk a Little While," a song written by one of the *Youngie* out in Colorado, he felt almost relieved. The stubborn *Maedsche* thought she'd make her point by zipping her lips, did she? Well, at least she had enough respect for the bride and groom to share in the singing and express her well wishes that way.

Old Order Amish churches like theirs didn't allow singing in parts during worship. In New Mexico, where he'd grown up, the *Ordnung* forbade it in any gathering. The bishop felt it was too showy, too likely to single out the better voices at the expense of the weaker, when all should be free to praise *Gott* in song. But since Seth's family had moved here to the Siksika Valley, Seth had noticed that the *Youngie* sometimes tried out harmonies at singings, or on special occasions like this one. He had a private theory that Little Joe Wengerd, the bishop, liked a bit of livelier music now and again, and appreciated the care that went into learning parts by ear.

After the cake was distributed and the singing concluded, the bride and groom went upstairs with their twins, Gracie and Benny, where they would spend their wedding night. Tobias and Sylvia were going to live here in the big house at the K Bar K Ranch with Josiah and Kathryn Keim. Josiah had already begun arrangements to make Tobias a partner in the ranch, while Stephen Kurtz stayed on as foreman. Josiah, Seth knew, was a smart man. With two capable men at the reins running one of the bigger ranches in the valley, he could ease out from under the heaviest of the workload. Sylvia would continue to keep the books and do the payroll and ordering, and in time she and his brother would inherit the ranch.

Seth sometimes wondered what it would be like to forge a path in life and know what was ahead of you. Tobias just seemed to do that naturally. Seth had concluded some time ago that he just didn't have that gift. Mostly he just caught a current in the river of life and went with it. Move from one state to another when Mamm got the notion to go? He went. Get a job cowboying on his uncle's ranch? Sure, why not?

Sometimes he looked at it as accepting *Gottes wille*. But sometimes he wondered if it wasn't something deeper in himself that was wary of being so foolish as to say, "I'm going to do this." *This* meant planning, and putting himself in the way of criticism, and standing up for his own decisions. It meant counting on something to happen as you'd planned, which was dangerous when things all too often were taken away. It was just easier to leave things up to *Gott* and be ready when the current changed.

Maybe not as satisfying as charting an actual course, but easier.

Closer to eleven o'clock that night, he joined the snack line for a bite before heading back to the Circle M Ranch. There would be a family cleanup crew hard at work here by five a.m. tomorrow, putting the barn and house to rights after the wedding, and loading the bench wagon to go to its next destination for church. But he and Gideon, as well as Tobias and Stephen, had cattle to manage, and in ranch country, everything revolved around that.

But first, a snack for the road.

A cluster of the *Youngie* were gathered around a massive bowl full of potato chips, with about six kinds of dips, cold meat left over from the day, and plates of cut vegetables. At the end of the table were the last of the wedding cakes, saved for anyone who had a spare inch of space left in their stomach.

"Seth, did you hear?" His sister Susanna waylaid him by the bean dip. "Our cousin Emily Kuepfer is in the group that's touring the national parks out here in the west. I just heard they're going to be at Glacier after roundup—close enough to visit. Isn't that *wunderbaar?*"

That Emily, she sure got around. Her family lived way out east on Prince Edward Island, where the Amish had settled over the last ten or fifteen years. The Kuepfers had visited at *Grischtdaag*, and the walls at the Circle M had practically bowed outward trying to contain all three families for Christmas dinner.

"What group is this?"

Susanna waved a potato chip laden with dip. "A bunch of *Youngie* hired a van and driver. She told me about it in one of her letters but I never thought they'd come this close. Emily and her friend from PEI. A few from Lancaster County, I think, including a married couple to chaperone. And some from Colorado, but I don't know who."

"That many people? In a van? For how long?"

"A big *Englisch* taxi-van. It must be pretty cramped. Emily said they were only allowed one bag for a trip that could be weeks."

His face must have reflected his horror, because Susanna laughed.

"The point is to get out and hike around the parks, *nix*? See scenery you've never seen before. Marvel at *Gott*'s handiwork. The van is just a means of getting from one park to the next."

And with her words, it dawned on him that by the time the van got here, roundup would be over, and he'd have his share of the cattle money in his pocket. His cousins Adam and Zach put every penny of their earnings toward the homes and lives they were building with the young women to whom *Gott* had directed them. Even Gideon had a future to think about these days, which he hadn't had at this time last year. But Seth?

Seth put his money in his bank account because he had nothing else to do with it. But he'd never seen much of the country. The move from the Ventana Valley to here. The occasional visit back east to Whinburg Township for family weddings and funerals. But that was mostly on the train, and you couldn't exactly get off and hike during stops. He of all his family was the easygoing one, the one that went along with things. The one who didn't get too attached, because you never knew when you were going to lose whatever it was—your father, your ranch home, your favorite horse, your favorite toy. Nothing lasted forever, even though you wanted it to.

Mamm would say that the only thing a person could depend on in this world was *der Herr*. He believed that. Seth sometimes felt he couldn't even depend on himself. What was he, after all? Just a cowboy, working on the Circle M until the next opportunity came along. He had a family he loved, but there was no special friend on the horizon. Never had been, really.

Standing there by the bowl of chips, he almost swayed at

the feeling that the current was changing. A prickle of excitement, of something almost like anticipation, tiptoed along his veins. What if ...?

"Is the van full?" he asked his sister. "Is that what everyone is talking about? That they want a seat?"

"I don't know," she said frankly. "But Emily said in her letter they were dropping two people off at Monte Vista. They might have picked up two people, for all I know. Why? Are you thinking of going?"

"Why not? Maybe the girl of my dreams is in that van."

Across the table of food, Beth Stolzfus rolled her eyes and took her plate over to where her sister Julie, her brother Alden, and his intended, Seth's cousin Malena Miller, were sitting.

Seth frowned after her. Why did Miss Grumpy have an opinion? What was wrong with doing something fun? Maybe this current he could practically feel moving around him was actually the hand of *Gott* giving him a little push. Maybe his flippant words were closer to the truth than he knew.

Well, Beth Stolzfus's opinions meant nothing to him. If the van full of *Youngie* rolled into the valley with an empty seat, he'd have his one bag packed, ready to roll out with it.

❧   2   ❧

SEPTEMBER 11

Off Sunday

THE VAN HAD ARRIVED yesterday after four days in Glacier National Park, and everyone had spent the night at the Circle M—the young men in the home of Daniel and Lovina Miller, overlooking the Siksika River, and the girls in the big house with his parents Naomi and Reuben. Most of the valley's *Youngie* found their way over there on off Sunday after lunch to hear all about it and to meet the travelers. Beth hung on every word that the tired but excited group had to share about their trip so far.

"I can't tell you how glad we are to be here," Emily Kuepfer said, pretending to sag against a post as the *Youngie* formed a conversation circle over by the pasture fence. "The van and Lori Turnbull, our driver, met us at the train station in Denver, so we didn't get to church until after that."

"We did sing the *Loblied* and read scripture before we left the motel," one of the girls reminded her. Delia, that was her name. She was the younger sister of Jeannie Kauffman, the married chaperone who looked barely older than Beth's sister. Jeannie was curvy and wore pink to church and had eyes that always seemed to hold a smile, even when she was serious. Maybe that was one of the reasons Chris Kauffman had fallen in love with her.

But what did Beth know about why people fell in love? The whole business was a mystery to her—love couldn't be trusted. Look at Mamm and Dat. They must have been in love when they got married, but by the time Beth was old enough to know that most husbands didn't *discipline* their wives as much as they did their children, it was long over with.

Discipline. She hated that word. It only appeared once in the Bible, but for all the times Dat said it, you'd think it was in the Israelites' mouths as often as the Lord's name.

She shook herself out of her unwelcome thoughts and back to the story. Janelle Stutzman, Emily's friend from PEI, took up the tale.

"We dropped off Jed and Moses King at their relatives' place in Monte Vista, then went to church in Amity, where Catherine Yutzy and her brother Carl joined us." The two of them smiled and gave a little wave to the group. They looked so similar with their blond hair and dimpled chins that Beth thought they might be twins.

Janelle went on, "Monday we took the northern route to Glacier, and my goodness—I thought I'd get a crick in my neck looking up at those mountains. I've never been anywhere but Ontario and the Island," she said, as though confessing some shortcoming. "They're both *gut* for farming."

"At least you've been to Canada," one of the boys joked. "I haven't." Beth couldn't remember his name, but he was one of Chris Kauffman's brothers, and they lived in Whinburg Township.

"But this is the first time I've been in the States," Janelle said. "It's just me and my dad now—he's a lighthouse keeper—so there isn't much money for traveling."

The boy nodded sympathetically—Jude, that was his name. Jude Kauffman. He took up the tale. "We had four days in Glacier. What a place to start! Do you think it will be all downhill from there?"

Beth chuckled, and after a second the others started to laugh, too. Jude glanced at her as though pleased she'd been the first to get the joke. That grumpy-pants Seth Miller hadn't got it at all, if his straight face was any indication.

"The mountains, the rivers, the animals!" Delia Wagler sighed. "My first time seeing a bighorn sheep. From inside the van, of course," she added hastily. "It stood right in front of us. Lori got pictures and posted them."

"*Some* of us have Facebook accounts," Emily said, looking innocent.

"Your *Ordnung* doesn't allow a phone?" Tim Eicher asked her.

She shook her head. "Only for business, and even then, only during business hours. I leave mine at work. Then it doesn't tempt me."

"So does my mother," Beth said. "She owns the quilt shop here."

"Your *mamm* is Rose Stolzfus?" Emily's blue gaze swung back to her. "I remember that from when we were here at Christmas. I'd sure like to talk with her today. If I'm never going to get married, I might buy into the quilt shop in Neverita. That's where we live. I love quilting—fabric—everything about it."

Never going to get married? A girl as pretty as Emily must just say things like that to be modest. "Mamm does, too. She says it's not really work when you're doing what you love."

"Cowboying is work," Seth said flatly. "Even when you love it, trying to find a newborn calf in a hundred acres of bush is no picnic."

"Especially coming home covered in calf splatter," Tim Eicher said with a laugh. "Say, how many empty seats are left in that *Englisch* taxi-van?"

"Just two," Delia said. She had the same sparkle in her eyes as Jeannie, and wore a golden yellow dress.

What must it be like, Beth wondered, to wake up to each day believing it was a gift to be joyfully accepted? Not that Beth didn't ... now. But there had been many a day when the appearance of the sun had made the child she had been tremble with dread, and wish fruitlessly for the safety of the dark.

An electric charge tingled along every vein in Beth's body as an idea ignited in her brain. What was she thinking? Right now ... this minute ... here was a gift of her own. An empty seat in the van. What might it lead to? More important, did she have the courage to accept such a gift?

Ach, ja, she did, for sure and certain.

"Can I come along?" Tim said. From his tone, Beth thought he might be joking.

Delia clapped her hands in delight. "Not that I have anything to say about it—Chris is the one to speak to. But can you get away at no notice, just like that?"

"Roundup is over," Seth Miller drawled. "Tim and I have our pay and a couple of weeks before it's time to start buttoning up the ranch for winter. Tim, I might just come with you and talk to Chris about that other open seat."

Heat flooded into Beth's cheeks. The nerve! Wouldn't you

just know it? The minute it entered a woman's head that one of those seats could be hers, a man came along to claim it as his own, just because he was a man.

Beth felt like a quail about to explode out of a hedge. But if Seth and Tim weren't setting off to find Chris Kauffman right this minute, then maybe she could. Nobody noticed when she melted away and hurried across the yard and up the steps to the house. Chris was likely over by the barn with the men, and there was no way Beth would interrupt him there. It wouldn't be fitting. But his wife could. If Mamm agreed that Beth could go.

She found Jeannie Kauffman in the kitchen with Naomi, Rachel, and some of the other married women, and here was Mamm, too.

Beth took her mother aside. "I want to go on the trip with the others in the taxi-van. Can I?"

Rose blinked at her, her mouth falling open. "You?" she said at last. "You want to drive for days, sleeping in a tent, galloping around the scenery like a mountain goat?"

"*Ja*. I do."

"Do you have any money to fund this adventure?"

Beth nodded. "Emily Kuepfer told us how much it cost. Gas, meals, a daily fee for Lori the driver plus her hotel and meals, and park entrance fees. Divided by eleven people, it comes out to be pretty reasonable. And I have it in the bank."

Her mother's gaze softened. "Are you sure, *Liewi*? This isn't like you. You're such a homebody. Julie, I could understand. But not you."

"Maybe I want to do something different for once. Meet new people. Do new things." When her mother only gazed at her, still a doubting Thomas, Beth pulled out the one possibility that might convince her. She lowered her voice. "There's no one for me in the valley, Mamm. And here on this trip are three young men. They're all from away, but…"

A pleat formed between Mamm's brows. "Taking a leaf from Sharon Keim's book, are you? I don't know if chasing boys all over the western states is the best way to find a husband."

"But what if this is *Gottes Hand* at work? What if this opportunity is from Him?"

After a moment, Rose said, "When do you have to let them know?"

"Right away. Tim Eicher and Seth Miller are already planning to ask. I need to beat them to it. Please, Mamm? Can we at least talk with Jeannie?"

Wouldn't you know it, the question dropped like a stone into one of those silences when conversation pauses.

"Talk with me about what?" Jeannie Kauffman smiled and came over to them, and while some resumed their conversation, others were clearly hoping to find out what Beth wanted. Because when you combined Jeannie the chaperone with Beth being driven to speak up in public, it could only mean one thing.

"*Mei Dochder* has taken it into her head to join your group of *Youngie*," Rose said. "I'm so surprised at the idea I don't know whether to say *ja* or *neb*."

"Well then, you'd better say *ja*, hey, Beth?" Jeannie's smile was like a sunbeam. "My husband has the final say, of course, but as far as I'm concerned, we'd love to have another girl along." She took Beth's arm and squeezed it as though passing on a confidence. "It keeps the boys in line when they know they're outnumbered."

Amish boys were always outnumbered by girls. It was just a fact of life that most of them had long ago accepted. Boys could pick and choose, and people like Sharon Keim were usually the ones who got chosen. People like Beth were often faced with life as a senior single, living at home and being the favorite *Aendi* of their siblings' children. Not that she was anywhere near that age yet—she was only twenty-two. But still. Twenty-two was the age when a woman wanted to be married, and Beth's prospects were thin on the ground.

"Will you talk to your husband for me?" she ventured. "And let me know? When do you leave?"

"We're heading for Yellowstone tomorrow," Jeannie said. "It's four hundred miles, so Lori wants to be on the road by seven at the latest."

"I can be ready, if Chris agrees," Beth said. Four hundred miles! She'd never been that far from her family before. For a moment, she almost backed out. Then through the kitchen window, she saw Tim and Seth ambling away from the circle of *Youngie*, and knew exactly where they were headed. "Can you ask him now?" she said urgently. "He's down at the barn, I think."

"Are you in that much of a hurry to see Old Faithful?" Jeannie asked with a laugh.

"Two of the boys were talking about asking him, too. But there's only two seats, and I want to be in one of them."

Jeannie nodded and patted her shoulder. "I see. Well, I do have a question for my *Mann*, so I'll just take a stroll and find him."

"*Denki*, Jeannie."

"Don't thank me yet. For all I know, he might have consented to two other people, and all three of you will be disappointed."

CHRIS KAUFFMAN WASN'T IN THE LANE, AND PROBABLY wasn't in the house visiting with the women. Seth figured he was likely down by the barn, where the Millers and their visitors were probably exchanging news and speculating on the likelihood of snow now that it was mid-September.

Jeannie Kauffman gave them a big smile as she passed them on her way up from the barn, where Seth could see Chris holding out one hand at shoulder height as though he was describing the size of something. When they joined the group of men, he found out he'd been describing a bighorn sheep. Seth had seen one himself, on his one and only trip to Glacier National Park when they'd first moved here, but it was fun to hear a man talk about his first sighting, too.

With a glance at Tim, he waited politely until Chris finished the story. Then he moved up beside the man and smiled. "You sound just like I did when I saw my first bighorn." He took a breath and jumped in. "I hear there's a couple of seats available when you folks pull out tomorrow. Any chance *mei freind* Tim and I might join you?"

A. pained look crossed Chris's face and Seth's stomach plunged. They were too late. "I'm afraid you'll have to arm-wrestle for the last seat, boys. My wife and I just promised the other one to someone else."

"Who?" Tim blurted.

"A girl. Name escapes me just now, but you can ask Jeannie."

"A girl," Seth repeated. Well, it could be worse. He glanced at Tim. "Maybe we can talk her out of it."

"Most of the girls around here have jobs," Tim said. "Who would just up and leave on a trip with no notice?"

"Your sister doesn't have a job," Seth pointed out. "It might be her."

Tim hooted at the very idea. "Ruthanne has enough to do helping us run the ranch, and Hope is barely old enough to start *Rumspringe*, never mind travel hundreds of miles by herself."

"Well, we have to find out. The sooner we convince her it would be better to stay home, the more time we'll both have to pack."

"One bag," Chris reminded him. "No room for anything more."

That was easy. Everything Seth possessed—except his saddle and tack and his boots—would probably fit in one bag.

When they got back to the circle of *Youngie* by the fence, they found it had grown. Sharon Keim and her sister had joined it, looking so excited that Seth's heart leaped. What if Sharon was the girl? *Oh please, please*, he begged Heaven wordlessly. Then he would only have to convince Tim to sacrifice his seat on the altar of love.

"I've never been so surprised in my life," Sharon was saying. "Hallo, Seth. Hallo, Tim. Did you hear?"

"Don't tell me," Seth said with his best smile. "You're joining the bunch in the taxi-van tomorrow."

Sharon laughed and waved the very idea away as though it were a fly. "Not me. I'm staying on the K Bar K until Aendi Kathryn pushes me out the door, or it starts to snow, whichever happens first."

"Well, who then?" Tim asked.

Which was good, because Seth couldn't get a word past the disappointment blocking his throat.

"Me," said a quiet voice.

Seth looked around, but couldn't see where it might have come from. Not Ruthanne. Was it Sharon's sister—or one of the Yoder girls?

Then Beth stepped out from behind Julie, who was shaking her head in disbelief. "Me," she repeated. "I'm going."

"*Wunderbaar!*" Emily clapped her hands and then pulled Beth aside. They plunged into a lively discussion of what she should pack in that precious single bag.

If Seth had been disappointed before, it was nothing to what he felt now. Beth? Little, mousy, silent Beth was going to take one of the seats in the van that should be his or Tim's or Sharon's? What would she do with herself? Sit there in silence and just occupy space until they'd seen the last park and were heading home? What was the point? She could stay home and do that.

"Seems a bit late to talk her out of it," Tim said in a low voice. "Guess we ought to find a couple of hymnbooks, get someone to put a straw in each, and see who draws the short one."

Startled, Seth stared at him. That was practically sacrilegious, imitating the process of choosing a bishop for something so trivial. Well, comparatively trivial. Nothing about this was trivial to Seth at the moment.

"There has to be something we can do," he said.

"Well, you and she don't get along. Everybody knows that. I'd be doing you a favor if I went. You wouldn't have to spend all those hundreds of miles locked in a van with her."

"Don't get along?" Seth repeated. "I say *guder mariye* when I shake hands after church, and *guder nacht* when she leaves after singing. How is that not getting along?"

But Tim only rolled his eyes. "We might be reduced to arm wrestling after all."

"Who's arm wrestling?" Jude Kauffman must have ears like a cat. "What are you wrestling over?"

"Who gets that last seat," Tim said easily, as though it

didn't matter. "We thought we were both going with you, but it looks like Beth beat us to it. One of us has to bow out."

"That's rough," Jude said sympathetically. Then he brightened. "You could have the wrestling match later. Maybe before singing, so we can all watch."

His brother Peter laughed. "Or maybe I should trade my seat for a saddle. Think you could teach me how to be a cowboy between now and tomorrow morning?"

The *Youngie* from the valley broke out in laughter at the joke. "There are some things that have to be lived, not taught," Seth told him, drawing on a significant well of experience. "Like how hard it is to walk after fourteen hours in the saddle."

"Or how ornery a horse can be when you want to tack her up in bad weather," Malena Miller said.

"Or how fast a calf can move when you're trying to cut him out from the cows," Adam Miller added.

Peter didn't look convinced, so Seth added some fuel to the fire. Flippantly, he said, "I'm just a hand here, so I can't speak for them. Maybe you should sweet-talk Tim's father."

"That's true," Tim said, as if he were really serious. "Dat will be down a hand, and roundup's over. Nothing to do around the ranch except repair tack and clear irrigation canals." Then he and Seth laughed. As if. There was always more work to do on a ranch than there were hours in the day to do it.

Much later in the afternoon, after coffee and plates of cake and cookies, and with the question of who was going still unresolved, Tim came and found Seth on the big deck out back with his family. They'd been talking over Mamm's wedding, which was coming up fast. He and Gideon were to be Luke's *Neuwesitzern*, since Luke's family was elderly and far away. Tim looked as though he'd been kicked by a calf.

Seth pulled him around the corner and leaned on the deck rail. "What's the matter with you?"

"He actually did it." At Seth's blank look, Tim blurted, "Pete Kauffman. He asked Dat if he could stay and learn some cowboying, and Dat said that as long as he didn't plan on being paid for the privilege, it was fine with him."

Pete's choices weren't the point here. Seth was looking at the horizon that had just opened up before him. "That means there's another seat. That we don't have to arm wrestle. We can both go tomorrow."

"I know. I already cleared it with Chris. He's wasn't as shocked as I am. Seth—that crazy kid is never going to make it even for a week on a cattle ranch. He has no idea."

"Then he can get on a train and be happy back in Whinburg Township." Excitement bubbled under Seth's breastbone. He, who hardly ever cared enough about anything to get worked up about it, was getting worked up about an empty seat in a van.

Ah, but it was much more than an empty seat. It was the adventure it represented. The unknown. What actually lay beyond the horizon. This time tomorrow, he could be standing in awe in front of Old Faithful. Or a real live buffalo. Or any number of amazing sights he didn't even know about yet.

Even the thought of Beth Stolzfus and her frowny face couldn't dim the rush of anticipation.

MONDAY, SEPTEMBER 12

7:00 a.m.

BETH COULDN'T QUITE BELIEVE she was here, less than a day after she'd made this crazy decision. For half that time, she'd been tempted to back out, and only the thought of what Seth Miller would say when he heard she'd caved after all kept her from actually doing it. But here she was, in the yard of the Circle M, having been collected by Tim and his older brother Samuel in the Eicher buggy. Pete Kauffman would ride back to the Eicher ranch with Sam.

"Bags in the rocket box," Lori Turnbull, the *Englisch* driver, instructed. "Then load up—we're moving out in ten minutes."

Beth tossed the backpack she'd borrowed from Julie to Chris, who stowed it in the van's rooftop carrier with the camping gear. Tim's bag followed it. Everyone staying at the Circle M had already loaded theirs. Then she climbed in and tried to get her bearings. There were eleven seats—one next to Lori, three opposite the sliding door, a single, then three with a space, then the back row of four.

"Doesn't matter where you sit, as long as it's with us." Emily claimed the three opposite the door, and Beth found herself on the aisle feeling as though everyone else had to climb over her in order to get farther back.

The only person who didn't was Seth, who was the last one in and took the single on the door side. He stretched out his long legs in satisfaction. "About the seventh hour, I'm going to appreciate this."

"Won't be worse than fourteen in the saddle," Tim observed from the back row with Chris, Carl Yutzy and Jude Kauffman. "These seats are pretty cushy."

"Everybody in?" Jeannie Kauffman thumped two big bags full of containers of food in the space next to Delia Wagler and Catherine Yutzy, who sat together. "We'll stop at the halfway point for lunch. You two—" She indicated Seth and Beth. "—are responsible for looking after these bags. Don't want the lunch provided by Naomi getting trampled at bathroom breaks."

Beth would rather have shared the task with Jude or Carl or even Tim Eicher, but it wasn't like she and Seth were roped together. And it was only for today.

"Ready?" A chorus answered in the affirmative. Lori climbed into the driver's seat, with Jeannie on the passenger side. "Nothing left behind? Purses, wallets, shoes and socks?"

"No!" came the response.

"All righty, then. Seat belts on, please, whenever the engine is running. Nobody sits here but me. Who's driven a car before? Anyone?"

They looked at each other, eyebrows raised. That was not a question Beth had been expecting—if it was possible to expect anything on such an adventure. Everything was likely going to be new to her.

Jude spoke up from the back. "I've driven a truck. On *Rumspringe*. But not since."

"Then in the case of dire emergency, if I'm unable to, you're the designated driver."

Jude made a kind of croaking sound. "But—but I'm baptized." And didn't have a driver's license.

"*Dire* emergency," Lori repeated. "I had a little talk with Reuben last night on the subject, and he felt that no bishop would condemn you if it meant saving a life or the safety of the whole group. A state trooper might feel differently, but I know which is more important to this group. Only if you're up for it, Jude. It's your decision."

"A-all right," Jude managed. "But I hope I won't need to."

"Me too," Lori told him. "Here we go."

Beth wondered if their driver had been around the Amish a fair bit, or was merely a fast learner, to be aware of the magnitude of what she was asking. But in a way, no matter how long it had been for Jude, it was kind of a relief to know someone could help if something happened to Lori.

Their driver wheeled the van around in the yard, and with the Miller family waving good-bye from the stairs, they were off down the lane in a cloud of dust, bound for Yellowstone National Park.

Beth had been in taxi-vans before, of course. But not one this big, and not one she'd be traveling in for at least two weeks. Somehow going sixty miles an hour instead of the trotting pace of a horse made the horizon bigger. Or maybe it just seemed that way because it was scrolling past at such a speed that new vistas opened up every couple of minutes.

The Circle M's last post at the property line flashed past, then the house and barns of the Bontrager place, then the *Englisch* ranch next to them, and in a minute the van was slowing for the town of Mountain Home. There was Mamm at the door of the quilt shop, waving good-bye for the second time that morning. Here came Alden out of the blacksmith shop to do the same, and then she saw Seth's family waving from the south-facing deck of the Wild Rose Amish Inn, just before they crossed the bridge.

Beth felt a lump rise in her throat. It was the first time in her life that she'd said good-bye to her family for more than a day, or at most a weekend with one of her buddy bunch back in Pennsylvania. She knew now what a comfort Ruth's whispered words must have been to her mother-in-law Naomi:

Entreat me not to leave thee, or to return from following after thee: for whither thou goest, I will go; and where thou lodgest, I will lodge. Thy people shall be my people, and thy God my God. Where thou diest, will I die, and there will I be buried: the Lord do so to me, and more also, if aught but death part thee and me.

The road south to Libby was a familiar sight, the trees just beginning to turn color. The aspens were always first, delicate things that they were, turning yellow-gold and standing out among the sober green of the pines. But Beth had never been south of Libby and its train station. As they descended out of the mountains, they were once again in rolling ranch country surrounding Flathead Lake. There was something comforting about country like this. Almost like home.

"Didn't expect to drive half the morning and wind up looking at what I left," Seth murmured to no one in particular.

"Oh, come on," Beth said, when no one seemed to have heard him. "Look at Flathead Lake. It's huge. Siksika Lake looks like a pond in comparison."

"Our mountains are a lot closer, though."

"If you're going to spend the trip comparing what you see to what you left behind," Jeannie said, turning her entire seat around to talk to them, "you might as well have taken a book out of the library. This trip is meant to be an adventure. So we can appreciate *Gott*'s creation just as we find it, not whether it measures up to what we already know."

"Hear, hear," Lori said, her eyes on the highway, both hands relaxed on the wheel.

Beth wondered if the driver's seat turned all the way around, too. Surely not. That didn't seem very safe.

"Where are we stopping for lunch?" Catherine asked with an air of changing the subject.

"Wherever we happen to be when it's time for *Middagessen*," Jeannie said cheerfully. "Keep an eye peeled for a nice view and a couple of picnic tables."

That turned out to be a highway rest stop somewhere past the halfway point, but it had restrooms and picnic tables and even a view. Beth had never been so thankful for Naomi Miller's provisions. Mamm had tucked one of Hezekiah Zook's little round cheeses into her purse with a plastic container of fruit and some muffins, but Beth decided to keep it until tomorrow. Who could turn down sandwiches layered with elk steak sliced thin, lettuce and tomatoes, and slathered with horseradish? Or barbecued trout mixed with mayonnaise? A plastic container held carrot-cake cupcakes with cream cheese frosting, and from an ice chest, Lori produced bottles of water.

"Traveling can dehydrate you," she told them. "We won't be drinking soda on this trip. Whether you like it cold or not, drink a bottle every two hundred miles or so. As you know, this is dry country."

Dry, but beautiful. Here, halfway to who knew what

wonders, Montana's famous big sky arched over their heads, and the sun felt warm on Beth's shoulders.

Emily got up to collect the paper plates and empty water bottles, so Beth joined her. It was an act so familiar it was comforting—taking the place of a servant so that she felt like part of the group, yet not standing out by actually speaking up. She might not have much conversation, but there were days and days of that ahead of them as they got to know one another.

"We need to establish a kind of schedule," Jeannie said, putting away plastic containers for washing later. "You see what Emily and Beth have begun? I've been on trips where certain people establish a way of doing things on the first day, and they do it for the whole trip. I'm pretty sure these two girls don't want to be cleaning up after all of you for three weeks."

Emily laughed, but Beth managed to say, "I don't mind."

"You might not right now, but by next week you will."

"But aren't we supposed to be servants to our brothers and sisters?" Seth Miller drawled.

The nerve of him! Did he want her on cleanup duty for the rest of the trip? He shouldn't mock the servant's place. It was not some false show of humility like he seemed to be implying with that tone.

"That's exactly what Jeannie is saying," Lori said, and a moment too late, Seth seemed to realize he'd fallen right into a trap. "Each of you will pick a partner for meal duty. Every meal, unless we're in a restaurant, of course, one pair will prepare it for the rest of us, and a different pair will clean up. I'll leave it up to you to figure out who and when."

"And be sure to sit in a different seat in the van each day— at least for the first week," Chris added. "That way, you'll have someone new to get to know. By the time we reach the train station to go home, you'll all be the best of friends."

Beth did not look at Seth, who was not by any stretch the best of friends. Just the thought of being trapped in the rearmost seat next to him was enough to give her the heebie-jeebies.

"Men on meal duty?" Tim Eicher said. "Seems like we'd be more useful doing something else."

"Time enough for that," Chris said. "Those who aren't cooking will be setting up the tents at our camp spots, and breaking them down the next morning."

"I don't know how to cook," Tim said flatly.

"But I'm sure you've been camping, or hunting with your father or *Onkel*."

"*Ja*, but—"

"So if you teach your partner how to manage a tent, I'm sure she'll teach you what to do when it's your turn to cook."

"Then I choose Delia." He grinned at her, clearly aware that she'd been camping in Glacier and knew what to do. Less work for him.

She grinned back, clearly delighted at the speed of *that* decision. "You don't know if I can cook," she teased.

"You probably know more than Seth here." Tim hooked a thumb at him.

"Hey! I can scramble eggs and cook bacon."

"*Gut*, then you're on for breakfast tomorrow."

Having been trapped twice in ten minutes, Seth implored patience from *Himmel* with a roll of his eyes.

If there were any young women in the group too shy to ask a young man to partner with them, it didn't matter. Seth looked in Emily's direction, only to find Jude Kauffman already asking her to be his partner to cook supper the following day.

Carl Yutzy snapped up Janelle Stutzman for tent duty, leaving Emily and his sister Catherine looking at each other and shrugging.

"I'm not going to let you partner with your cousin Seth," Catherine told her. "That defeats the purpose. Besides, tents are a lot simpler than cooking. We don't need a man to help us do that."

Beth was so busy watching this game of musical chairs that she didn't realize that she was the last to pick a partner. In slow motion, her gaze swung to the only candidate left.

Who needed a partner to cook breakfast.

Ach, neh. This can't be happening.

SINCE THEY'D HAD A LONG DRIVE, THE GROUP AGREED unanimously with Chris's suggestion that for this first supper, they find a restaurant and eat before they entered West Yellowstone and found the Madison campground. There wasn't a table for twelve available, and when they split up to various tables they collected a few stares from the tourists eating dinner, but Seth told himself he'd get used to it. Cattle and horses didn't care that he was Amish, but from the surreptitious use of cell phones, quite a number of *Englisch* did.

Beth Stolzfus sat at a table for four with three other girls. At no time since her brief agreement to be his partner for breakfast had she spoken to him. Or even looked at him. Which was fine. There was plenty to look at out the window.

After a quick stop for a few groceries, they entered the park at last just as the sun was gilding the tops of the pines. When they reached the Madison campground, Seth climbed out of the van and took a deep breath.

He loved the smell of pine, though these were different from the ones at home. Out of the corner of his eye, he saw Beth doing the same thing, breathing it in and gazing in what looked like delight toward the river bending through the meadows visible through the trees.

Suddenly a sound echoed in the distance. "What was that?" Janelle Stutzman said on a gasp. "Was it a bear?"

There must not be any bears on Prince Edward Island.

Beth shook her head reassuringly. "*Neh*, that was an elk. Once you hear that sound, you never forget it."

"And since this is a national park, they don't have to be afraid of hunters," Seth added, wondering where she'd heard an elk bugling. Then again, elk lived around the Siksika and all through the Kootenai—they just headed for the high country during hunting season. He'd heard them himself during roundup. And she was right—it was a pretty distinctive sound.

"Come on, time to set up," Chris said as Lori used a key to open the rooftop storage container. "Tent helpers, men sleep in one of the big ones, *Maedscher* in the other. Jeannie and I will set up our two-person honeymoon suite. People who aren't setting up tents get to blow up mattresses."

"Lori, where are you sleeping?" Emily asked their driver shyly.

The *Englisch* woman smiled. "I'm no fan of sleeping on the ground. Not since I turned fifty. This van is a wonder—the back seats drop down to form a bed. That'll be mine for the duration."

"So the food will go in the van with you?" Jude asked.

"What, you think I want to be dinner for a bear, gift wrapped in a tin can?" She laughed. "Nope. Food will go in the bear box."

"So there *are* bears," Janelle said.

"Not around here so much, but in the park, yes," Lori told her. "If you go hiking, stick to the marked trails. No rambling off into the woods, and no carrying food in your pockets."

"I promise," she said faintly. Definitely having second thoughts, and it was only the first day.

Seth got busy with the air mattresses, which came with a handy pump. Not the electric kind, the foot-pedal kind, but it was better than the lung kind. He, Carl, and Jude took turns pumping. In surprisingly short order, the dome-shaped tents were set up and secured, and the girls carried the mattresses in and unrolled the sleeping bags.

"I notice that all the men brought their own sleeping bags," Jeannie said, arranging her own tent with the ease of experience.

"Comes of all those hunting trips," Chris reminded her. "Fewer for our *Youngie* to borrow, *nix?*"

Once camp was set up, they were free to explore. Carl and Catherine headed for the river, and Beth went with them. Seth figured maybe he should go, too. Walk off that hamburger and fries. And maybe he could talk Beth out of breakfast duty. She could trade with one of the other girls. After all, he and she knew each other. If this partnering-up business was match-making in disguise, then he and Beth should certainly split up.

The other three made their way through the tall grass, respectfully keeping downstream of the *Englisch* fishermen casting farther up.

"I should have brought my rod and reel," Carl said. "Never even thought of it. Instant supper."

"Five fish won't go far with twelve people." Beth glanced up. "Didn't you hear those men talking behind us at the restaurant? Limit of five, and brookies only."

"Guess we'll have to remember that for next time," Seth

said easily. "If you trust the eavesdropping method of learning the regs."

Beth moved away, and he realized too late that his attempt at humor had fallen flat. She knelt on the bank and waggled her hand in the water. With a gasp, she snatched it out, then put it in again.

"What's the matter?" Catherine wanted to know. "Are the fish biting?"

"It's *warm*. Come and feel."

"We must be downstream of the Firehole," Carl said. "That's why they call the river that—the water is warm."

"Oh, how I wish I had a bathing suit," Beth said on a sigh. "I'd just slide right in like it was a bathtub."

Seth's eyebrows went up as he resolutely shut the door on any possible image of any girl he knew doing such a thing.

"Why don't you have one?" Catherine asked curiously. "Your *Ordnung*?"

Beth nodded. "If we really want to swim, we put on an old dress and pin the skirt up the middle." She shot a glance at Seth. "Not like the boys, who go skinny dipping when they think nobody's looking."

"Sometimes after roundup, the river is the only way to get all the trail dust and calf spatter off," he said. "And the Siksika is always either just thawing or about to freeze. No warm water in sight. Kind of takes the fun out of it."

Catherine pretended to shiver. "Come on, let's wade. We might not get another chance." She was already pulling off her sneakers and socks.

After a moment, Beth did the same, and Seth couldn't resist the chance to feel a warm river for the first time in his life. Soon the four of them were wading as far out as they dared, trying to stay out of the deeper channel in the middle.

"I hope no one is trying to fish downstream of us," Carl said, his pants rolled up as far as they would go.

"We'll herd everything toward them if there are," Beth said cheerfully, her tanned feet wavering under the water, her green skirts gathered up in both hands.

Carl and Catherine were soon ahead, looking for smooth stones to skip. Seth seized his chance, his longer wading stride catching up with Beth's shorter one in a couple of steps.

"I was thinking about tomorrow's breakfast," he said in a friendly tone.

"You just had supper." She bent over, looking at something underwater he couldn't see.

"I mean, about us making it. I wondered if maybe you'd rather trade with one of the other girls."

She straightened, dragged her gaze off whatever was so fascinating down there, and her puzzled eyes found his. "Why? You know I can cook. You've been to all the same potlucks and fellowship meals I have."

"It's not about the cooking." He hesitated, then decided to be honest. "If the point of all this partnering up is to get to know the others, then it's a missed opportunity if we partner with someone we already know."

She stared at him, adjusting her stance against the push of the current. "You want someone else to cook with you."

"I have no problem cooking with you. I just think that if—"

"*Ja*, I heard you. But if there's someone you'd rather be with, that's fine with me. I'll trade with them." She turned her back on him, swinging around to look downstream for the others.

A stone turned under her bare foot—he heard it grind against its neighbor—and in the space of a blink, she lost her balance. With a splash, she landed in the deeper channel in the middle and went under.

Arms and legs flailed, and her face surfaced just long enough to let her choke out a shriek before the current swept her past him and she went under again.

Seth moved as though galvanized by a cattle prod. Two long strides and he dove full length into the current, those long childhood days swimming in the Chama River coming back to him as though it had been only yesterday.

She had sunk into the deeper water, the current wanting to bowl her down the channel like a ball. No time to figure out arms or legs—he grabbed the first thing he saw. Her dress, billowing. Hauling her in like the disciples must have hauled in their catch on the other side of the boat, he kicked off the bottom and pulled her into shallower water. Turning her on her hands and knees, he did what his cousin Zach had once done after pulling someone out of Siksika Lake, and relief cascaded through him as she coughed up the water she'd ingested.

It wasn't pretty, and she was crying, but she did it.

"Come on, let's get you back to camp." Before she could protest, he swung her up into his arms and strode with her across the sandbar to where the bank sloped up to a viewing bench. For someone who only came up to his shoulder, she was solidly built, and it was all he could do to make it up the gentle slope without going to his knees and dumping her in the dirt. Their camp was two spots down, and Chris was already running to meet them.

"What happened?"

"Fell in," Seth said curtly as he reached their campsite. "Sucked in a bunch of water. Need a towel."

"Put me ... down." Beth pushed at his shoulders, coughing, crying, water dribbling everywhere.

"Can you stand?"

She didn't answer, but he let her slide down until her bare feet touched the pine needles. He expected her knees to buckle, but they didn't. She stood as though held up by sheer will, and released his arm, clutching the end of the picnic table instead.

"Here, Beth." Jeannie engulfed her in a towel and rubbed briskly. "Lori, see if you can find her backpack. It's dark blue with white piping. She'll need dry clothes."

Seth waited while the two women took her into the girls' tent, and in ten minutes they reappeared, with Beth now in a dress the color of madrone bark, breathing easier and combing out her wet hair. Chris had already rigged up a clothesline between two trees, and Jeannie draped the wet dress over it. But Seth was only dimly aware of it.

His whole attention was absorbed in the sight of Beth Stolzfus combing out hair that fell to her waist, as brown and sleek as an otter's pelt. It wasn't as though he'd never seen Mamm and Susanna after washing theirs. Same with his aunt and cousins at the Circle M. But this was different. Amish women never let down their hair in public. Even little girls didn't. It was hypnotizing.

The sun chose that moment to find its way through the ranks of pines and touch her with a golden column of light. The warmth of it—the dry air—sped up the drying process and her hair began to develop waves.

"Where is your *Kapp?*" Jeannie said, joining her on the picnic bench.

The rhythm of the comb's strokes faltered. "I—don't know. I must have lost it in the river. I didn't think to tie the strings."

"Do you have another?"

"I didn't think I'd need more than one." Her face crumpled. "I didn't expect to go swimming. It's probably back in Montana by now."

Seth collected himself with a jolt. An Amish woman couldn't go three weeks with only a *Duchly*—a kerchief—to cover her head. "I'll go look for it. There's a lot of overhanging brush—it might have got caught in something."

He loped back down the slope, which was a little muddy from the cascade of water they'd left behind. He waded in, eyed the current and the formation of channel and sandbars, and made his best guess about where the stream might have taken something as light as a *Kapp*. At least, he hoped its stiffness might have made it behave like a little boat instead of collapsing like a dishcloth and going to the bottom.

"Where's Beth?" Carl Yutzy called, emerging from around a bend with his sister. "Did she have enough?"

"She fell in." Explanations could wait until later. "She lost her *Kapp*. Come and help me look for it."

A quarter of an hour later, Catherine exclaimed in triumph from behind a deadfall. "Got it!" She waved something white that no longer resembled the stiff, pleated bucket shape of the Siksika Valley Amish *Kapp*. Beth would know what to do about that.

But at least she wouldn't have to go before the Lord in a cotton scarf. Seth collected her sneakers and socks from the bank and walked into the campsite feeling like a fisherman who'd just bagged his limit.

$\mathscr{H}$ 4 $\mathscr{H}$

POOR *KAPP*. Without its starch, it made a very sad sight, and was dirty besides. But Beth took it from Catherine with glad thanks, and her sneakers and socks from Seth with a murmured, "*Denki*, Seth. I couldn't remember where I'd left them."

"No wonder." He paused. "You put your hair back up. And found a *Duchly*."

Startled, her eyes met his. "Well, sure. I couldn't very well walk around the camp with it blowing around catching bugs."

"I know. I'd just never seen it down, that's all. It was pretty."

And he strolled away to help Chris build the campfire, leaving Beth wondering if he'd been replaced by an identical twin. A much nicer identical twin.

She got busy with a small plastic washtub and dish soap, and while she scrubbed the sand and mud out of her *Kapp*, she had a few minutes to think. To remember. To briefly wonder what would have happened if Seth hadn't been there to grab her. Her mind shuddered away. She'd never learned to swim.

Unlike some of the *Youngie* in the valley who chafed against the pin-your-dress-together rule before they could swim, she'd never wanted to at all. From the few words that Alden and Mamm had dropped in her hearing, she suspected that something had happened when she was a toddler, leaving her with an aversion to being engulfed in water.

Bathtubs for some reason didn't bother her a bit. But lakes and rivers? She was happy to wade and paddle, *denki*, nothing more.

And now, here was Seth, his own clothes drying on him now that the fire was going, diving in to grab her before the current took her even farther away. She could barely bring herself to think of it—the way the water had roared in her ears, the way it had bowled her along the bottom like a rag doll, the way she couldn't control her body no matter how hard she tried. In the end, she thought she'd caught on a snag and would drown under some heavy dead tree. The terror had begun to claw its way up her throat—and there was Seth, reeling her in and helping her to the bank. Carrying her to safety—and she was no slender fairy like Sharon Keim.

And now giving her a compliment! In a day of unfamiliar signs and wonders, that capped the globe.

Emily appeared at her side as she inspected her wet *Kapp*. "How is it looking?"

"Cleaner," Beth said. "But I don't think it will ever be white again."

"No one expected us to bring along a fresh one for every day of the week. Or a bottle of bleach and spray starch. I expect all of ours will wind up the same way by the end of the trip."

Somehow, the thought was almost comforting. That they

would all be in the same boat, and she would no longer stand out.

"That was quite the rescue," Emily said casually. "For a man you say doesn't like you, he dove in fast enough when you were in trouble."

The tale was growing taller by the minute. "Did you see it?"

"Not the diving in, just the carrying out. Janelle and I were on the bank just above." She bumped Beth's shoulder gently with her own. "It was *very* romantic."

"Oh, good grief." Beth rolled her eyes and tried to reshape the *Kapp* with one hand inside it. "Please don't say that out loud."

"All right. But Catherine saw it, too. She was telling Delia all about it a minute ago. Seth is either going to get a swelled head or a special friend out of this."

If that was what it took to impress some girls, they were welcome to him. All she had to offer was actual gratitude.

"Do you think that if I dry this near the fire, it will be wearable by tomorrow?"

"It's what I would do. The material for this style is pretty stiff on its own. Be glad you don't wear a Lancaster County one, like Delia and the Kauffmans. It probably would have got torn to bits."

Beth nodded—both for the tearing to bits part and the glad she didn't wear one part. She and Julie had ditched their heart-shaped Lancaster County *Kapps* almost as fast as Mamm had. She'd been only too glad to adopt the valley's bucket-shaped design, though it had felt strange at first. New *Kapp*, new *Ordnung*, new home, new identity.

New Beth.

She'd grown into herself since then, though the shadows of the past still fell across her path when she least expected them.

Like today, in the water. And yesterday, feeling Seth's jokes as though they were arrows meant to wound.

The way her father's had. They'd always found their mark. She'd been the roly-poly child, never as quick as Julie, never as smart as Alden. Never good enough. Never able to measure up.

She shook off the shadows and took the *Kapp* over to the fire. "Can I bake this for a little while?"

"Sure." Seth had set up some folding stools, the kind shaped like an *X* that rolled up into easily packable tubes. Everything that Lori had in the van was compact and efficient, even with a group as large as theirs. She sat on one and held out her poor *Kapp* to the flames.

The others wandered back in ones and twos to join the few at the fire. The lid of the bear box gave a *thunk* as Chris closed it on tomorrow's groceries. The warmth of the fire felt *gut* on her face and hands as she patiently shaped the *Kapp* as it dried. Finally, it was dry enough for her to put it on and tie its strings, where hopefully it would remember the shape of her head before she took it off to sleep.

"Are you all right now, Beth?" Delia asked across the snapping flames.

"*Ja, denkes*. I'm very grateful to Seth for fishing me out like a great big trout." She hesitated. "I don't know how to swim. It was terrifying."

"Maybe some lessons are in order on this trip," Jude suggested. "I can teach you. I taught all my brothers and sisters."

That would be the day. But it was kind of him to offer. "Maybe."

"Or maybe she'd rather not," Emily said. "If a person didn't grow up around the water, there'd be no reason for them to learn to swim."

"Unlike us," Janelle said with a grin. "I was born in Ontario next to a lake so big you can't see the other side. Then we moved to an island surrounded by ocean. Water comes naturally to some, and not to others. *Gott* made us different to keep life interesting."

Tonight, in the privacy of the tent, Beth would thank them both for coming to her rescue, even if they didn't know it. The absolute last thing she wanted was to learn to swim.

They took turns telling riddles, and stories, and played Truth or Dare, which Beth and Janelle declined, but which resulted in Seth being dared to arm wrestle Tim Eicher on the picnic table, to the accompaniment of cheers and shrieks of laughter. Then, to everyone's surprise, Jeannie brought out the ingredients for s'mores. Beth had had them before, but there was something even more delicious about them tonight. Maybe it was the tang of the pines in the air that made them taste so good. Maybe it was the camaraderie and the fellowship of this group that hailed from so many places.

Or maybe it was because after the arm wrestling, Seth hadn't resumed his seat next to Delia, but kept busy stoking the fire and piling wood for tomorrow morning. He was so occupied that he didn't have time to make a s'more for himself. So instead of eating her first one, Beth got up and took it to him, hot and melting in her fingers.

"Denki," he said in surprise, dusting off his hands and biting into it. "Mmm. *Ischt gut.*"

"I think there's something in the air," she said lightly, thankful the twilight was too deep for him to see her blush. "People say hunger makes the best sauce, but Mamm always says it's gratitude that gives it flavor. I'm—I'm grateful for what you did today."

In the silence, she heard Delia laugh over the pop of pitch in the fire.

"Some guys might say it was nothing, but I won't," he said at last. "I didn't realize you couldn't swim."

She shook her head. "It was something." Then it occurred to her she'd forgotten to do what she'd said she'd do. It took the friendliness right out of the moment. Taking a step back, she said, "I was so *verhuddelt* I forgot to find you a partner for tomorrow. Give me a minute."

"*Neh*—Beth, wait."

She hesitated, gazing at him over her shoulder.

"I take it back. I don't want to change partners."

Did he mean it? After all he'd said about not wasting time with somebody he already knew and had written off his list? Well, he hadn't said that exactly, but that's what it boiled down to.

"Are you sure?"

"Certain sure." He grinned. "Because it will take more than gratitude to make anything I cook taste *gut*. Our friends here probably have higher standards than ranch hands do."

She couldn't help it. That grin was infectious and she smiled back despite the questions flapping in her mind like startled birds. "I can't say I've taught all my brothers and sisters how to cook, like Jude has taught all his how to swim, but I guess I could give you a lesson, if you wanted."

"Then everyone else will have some gratitude to flavor their food with. See you at six."

She nodded, and turned away. When she reached the fire and found Emily looking at her oddly, she realized that she was still smiling.

Tuesday, September 13

5:50 a.m.

Thank goodness there was coffee.

Beth buried her nose in a cup of steaming brew, to which she'd added one precious dollop of cream. Half a cup was enough to get her mind turning, like a buggy wheel coming out of the mud in which it had been stuck. By the time she'd downed the rest, she felt almost human.

It was a small price to pay, though, for staying up late around the fire. She'd heard Julie in her head saying, "Beth, you won't be able to function if you don't get some sleep," but she'd ignored her, listening instead to the talk around the fire, the stories ranging from childhood to travel, from favorite animals to *Ordnung*. It was like this on Sunday nights at home, and at volleyball games on Friday nights, too, she knew that. But it had been different last night.

Last night she had participated. They were all on an adventure together. It wasn't real life. It was like stepping on to the carousel at the fairgrounds, climbing on a painted horse, and being swept away into its world of light and color and music.

She'd shared a little, and found that both Delia and Jude knew some of the same people her family did. And Delia went to church with Melvin and Carrie Miller, who were Seth's cousins. Among the Amish, family and friendship connections formed a web, so that a person never really felt alone no matter how far they traveled.

So it had been worth it, even if she'd awakened this morning feeling every bruise from the rocks on the river bottom, and every hour of sleep she'd lost.

"*Kapp* looks good as new," Seth said, taking her cup and refilling it before she even asked.

"It's as good as it will get," she allowed, adding cream and resolutely putting the container back in the cooler. "All right. Let's get started. I hear people waking up."

Murmurs came from the tents. "Who will the sleepyheads be?" Seth wondered aloud. "Who will get a dunk in the river to wake them up?"

"You wouldn't," she said, laying out the bacon and opening the carton of eggs.

"I guarantee it won't happen again."

"Sounds like the voice of experience. As the dunker or the dunkee?"

"Let's just say the water then wasn't nearly as warm as our swimming hole here." He leaned over the picnic table to see what she was doing. "Are you going to teach me to make biscuits?"

"First you have to learn timing. Bacon takes the longest. If you fry up these two pounds, then I'll make a pan frittata with half these eggs. While it's cooking, I'll mix up the biscuits, and then fry the rest of the eggs while you bake the biscuits over the fire."

His eyebrows rose. "That sounds complicated."

"It takes a bit of planning to get everything on the table at once. That's why I'm glad there are two of us. We have both the fire and the Coleman stove, so we can do it easily."

One thing about Seth, he took instructions well. Was that the result of so many years of cowboying? Out on the trail, she knew that sometimes things could turn on a dime and result in injury to both man and beast. A person would have to have their wits about him and pay close attention to what a more experienced man told him to make sure everyone came home safely.

When they laid breakfast on the table and waved at everyone to come and sit down, she glanced at him and found that grin lighting up his face again. "Done and dusted," he said. "Just don't look at those first biscuits. I'm going to eat them."

"Butter hides a multitude of sins," she assured him.

During their silent grace, she thanked the *gut Gott* for her helper and his willingness to take the place of a servant. When everyone raised their heads, Lori smiled and passed her plate for a helping of the frittata, which Beth had flavored with onions, red peppers, and some poblano chiles she'd had Seth roast over the fire before she chopped them and tossed them in.

"This is *wunderbaar*," Chris said with his mouth half full. "What's in this egg pie?"

Seth told him about the secret of roasted chiles. "Beth must have got the recipe from my mother—when you live in New Mexico, chiles are like green beans in Pennsylvania. Plentiful and in everything."

"I did, in fact," Beth told them. "When we moved west, I discovered I like spicy food. We never ate it when we lived in Whinburg Township, but in the Siksika, I think the Miller influence is responsible for a lot. I even keep chile plants in the kitchen window, where it's warm enough for them to grow."

Beth enjoyed the fruits of her and Seth's labor almost as much as he seemed to. The glow of a job well done lingered even while they did the dishes. The cast-iron frying pan was a chore, but it had done its duty by both bacon and frittata perfectly, so she wouldn't complain about having to scrub it out afterward.

"Sure beats tent duty," she murmured to Seth, who was drying as fast as she washed.

"Carl is having a bad day," Seth said. "Last one up—I didn't have the heart to toss him in the river, though. His *Schweschder* embarrassed him enough, going into the men's tent and dragging him out of bed."

But somehow Carl kept a sense of humor about it all, and vowed to go to bed early that night. Beth would have been hiding her face in embarrassment, but he just made jokes at his own expense.

Today's adventure was to see Old Faithful and to find out what *mud pots* and *fumaroles* were. Beth had seen pictures of Old Faithful, but there was a lot more to this park than that. Lori told them a little about what caused the boiling-hot pools and the geysers, but it wasn't until they'd parked and set off along the boardwalks above the geothermal field that Beth really understood what she was seeing.

"Do you think the lake of fire is like this?" Delia whispered to her. "Do you think it smells this bad?"

"It's sulphur, and yes, I think the Bad Place does smell this bad," she whispered back. "Do we have to think about an eternal future when the ancient past is right in front of us and still alive?"

"Good point," Delia admitted. "Look at the colors in that mud pot. Turquoise, yellow, orange. *Gott* was having fun finger-painting in that one."

But Old Faithful was the sight of the day. Somehow the park employees knew exactly what time it was going to erupt, and people gathered around what looked like a mild bump on the ground. Steam issued out of it, but steam was coming out of the ground for as far across the field as she could see.

And then something changed. A small plume of boiling water went up. Another—a breath—and Beth gasped as the geyser shot into the sky, higher than a barn, higher than she would ever have believed. It fountained up, steam billowing, for one minute, two, acting like a pressure valve and emptying itself out ... then seemed to calm. The plumes became shorter, smaller, until at last only the steam was left, dwindling down to the height of all the others.

"Holy smokes." The elders back in Whinburg Township used to frown on that expression, fearing that it might somehow refer to the Holy Spirit, but it was the only one that conveyed her awe and even a tiny bit of fear.

"I'll say." She came back to herself to realize that Seth and Tim Eicher were standing on her other side, eyes wide and mouths open. "I wonder what *der Herr* was thinking when He created—" Seth waved at the geysers and the plumes of steam. "—this."

But there was no way to answer that. Beth wondered if Seth thought about things like that when he was riding fence or looking for calves during roundup.

Maybe somewhere along the road she'd gather the courage to ask him.

WEDNESDAY, SEPTEMBER 14

THE NEXT DAY, Lori took them on a tour of the park in the van. Seth soon lost track of which geyser field was called what, and Jude's attempt to count elk was equally short-lived once a herd traveled through one of the meadows and streamed across the road, bringing traffic to a halt. Nobody could count the moving animals fast enough. The van's route was roughly circular, up the west side of the big lake, then up to Mammoth Hot Springs and south again.

He would never have believed that driving around could make a man so tired. Or maybe it was the lack of sleep. And the sheer acrobatics of climbing in and out of the van every few miles to marvel at the scenery or the animals.

"We'll save the south entrance for tomorrow," Lori said as the turnoff for their campground came into view in the late afternoon. "We have a long driving day—nine hours at least from Grand Teton to Arches. Breakfast at six, break camp, and on our way by seven, all right?"

But in the early evening, around the fire, no one seemed to care about going to bed. Instead, Jeannie made hot chocolate, and Delia delivered steaming cups two at a time. She was just approaching Beth, walking carefully so as not to spill, when her toe caught on a root. Staggering, she let out a cry as half the piping-hot contents of the mug sloshed out onto her hand. She dropped both cups and, weeping with pain, hardly knew which way to turn for help.

Before anyone could move, Beth leaped up, grabbed her good hand, dragged her over to the Coleman, where a pot of cool water was waiting for the morning. She plunged the burned hand into it and Delia wailed, "Butter! You're supposed to put butter on it."

"*Neh*, you are not," Beth told her with quiet firmness. "The burn is going down into your skin. The water will stop it. Just keep it in there. Move it gently, like this. Is this the hand you write with?"

"N-no."

"That's a blessing." She looked up. "Emily, there's a pouch in the outside pocket of my backpack. Can you bring it here?"

Drawn by curiosity as well as concern, Seth hovered on the far side of the picnic table. He'd seen many a burn treated, but not so fast or so calmly. And he'd always thought you were supposed to put butter on one, too.

Fifteen minutes later, Beth helped Delia dry her hand with a clean dish towel, then gently applied the cure-all he'd seen his cousins use on visits to Pennsylvania. It was called Burn & Wound for good reason, and every Amish store stocked it. In the mystery pouch there was also a roll of bandage. She wrapped Delia's hand and sat back with a satisfaction.

"You should be all right in the morning, but we'll put some more B&W on it then, just to be sure. Do you want some hot chocolate? The girls have already washed the cups you dropped."

"*Neh*, I've lost my appetite for it," Delia said. "*Denki*, Beth. How did you know how to do all that? And who travels with a first aid kit in their backpack?"

"I do," Lori said, leaning on the van's bumper with a cup of hot chocolate cradled in her hands. "But nobody seemed to need me sticking my nose in. Nice work, Beth."

Beth flushed and ducked her head. "I want to be an EMT," she said in a low tone. "It was in the books I've been reading. What to do."

Seth's mouth fell open. "*You're* studying to be an EMT?"

The group by the fire had figured out something was going on now. A couple of them got up and moved closer to hear.

"I—well, not yet. I talked to Adam and Zach about signing up for the course they took, and Zach lent me a couple of his books." She bit her lip, then took a breath as though making up her mind. "I think he thought they would scare me off, but it was kind of the opposite."

"Does Rose know about this?" Seth blurted. "And Alden and Julia?"

"They might have seen me reading *Emergency Care and Transportation*. I didn't hide it. But I read a lot of stuff. They've stopped paying attention, mostly."

"But—you're a *Maedsche*," Carl said. "How can a woman be an EMT?"

"There's an Old Order Mennonite woman who's an EMT in our volunteer fire department in Lancaster County," Jude put in unexpectedly. "She doesn't drive the ambulance, but she does everything else the *Englisch* men do."

"Our *Ordnung* would never allow it," Janelle said, shaking her head. "No Amish man at home would think of it to begin with, never mind a woman."

"I don't think there are too many Amish EMTs, and I don't

know of any female ones," Tim said. Then he amended, "Except Sara Miller."

"Seth's cousin Sara never gave up her license." Beth's gaze flicked to Seth, as if for corroboration. "I've been talking to her, too. Once the baby comes, she won't be able to do it anymore ... but she said the fire captain would welcome a replacement."

"Sara jumped the fence and was an EMT in Washington State," Seth explained to the *Youngie* from away. "When she came back and joined church, our bishop thought it would be *gut* for our volunteer fire department to have an Amish woman EMT on call, even if she wasn't on a regular shift like my cousins."

"If a woman was in labor, or a little *Kind* was in trouble," Beth concluded with a nod. Then she hesitated. "I may not make it through the course. I'd have to take the exams on the computer, at the library. But Zach and Adam said if I was serious, they'd coach me."

"Wow," Emily said, her eyes wide. "How brave you are."

Silently, Seth wondered if that was true. Brave, or—well, he wouldn't say unwomanly, because she wasn't that—but this proved she wasn't exactly like any Amish girl he'd ever met. Quietly going about doing something so unusual you could probably count the others in the country on the fingers of one hand. And here he'd thought she was just a shy little mouse, hardly opening her mouth. So unobtrusive she'd never even been courted, never mind kissed.

His galloping thoughts skidded to a halt, like a horse spotting a rattler in the path.

Why are you even putting Beth *and* kissed *together in the same sentence? Are you crazy? Besides, what business is it of yours what she does?*

Beth Stolzfus was nowhere near his type. Sharon Keim, now, she was a different matter. He took refuge in that familiar dream. She'd been on so many dates that he had no doubt she knew her way around a kiss. And her willowy blond looks were exactly his type. She giggled a lot, that was true, but better a girl who saw the funny side of life than someone who just frowned at it from the shadows.

But what about a tourniquet? Does Sharon know her way around that?

What would a man need more in life—a smile and a kiss or a tourniquet? Huh?

But his ornery brain had no answer to that one, and Seth turned toward the fire. Not as though he was walking toward it for any reason, but feeling the need to walk away.

6:45 a.m.

Since Seth and Beth had been on the cooking crew yesterday, they were tent crew this morning. Even though she'd had her coffee and presumably a longer night's sleep, he'd noticed she was as silent as she was at home, as though the revelations of yesterday had taken something out of her. Or given her something to think about. He couldn't really tell which.

But because he was trying to figure her out, he wasn't paying all that much attention to what he was doing. From inside the men's tent, Carl whooped and without warning, the whole tent collapsed on him.

"Wrong pole," came a muffled voice from under the flailing weatherproof fabric while everyone laughed and Seth lifted it off him.

"Sorry, *mei freind*, I should have been in there helping you with it."

Carl waved off his apology and Seth buckled down to work. Words, after all, didn't mean much in Amish life. Actions did. Which meant they had the tent folded up and in its bag in the rocket box in no time, and they both had first pick of seats in the van. Seth kind of liked the single next to the door, because it had a big window and he could stretch out, but there were more young men with long legs in the group than just him. Not to mention he had to remember the suggestion about changing seats every day.

Well, someone had to sit in the very back. The other guys had had their turns, so he supposed it was his. Wouldn't it have been great if Sharon Keim had come along? Then he could be perfectly happy back here, cuddled up beside her, talking quietly about the sights along the way for nine hours.

He was happily enjoying this dream when Janelle and Emily climbed in beside him, Jude bookending them. Beth sat in the seat ahead of him with Carl Yutzy beside her and his sister on his other side. With a grin of triumph, Chris claimed the single for his wife, and when she was comfortable, he went up front to the passenger seat next to Lori. Tim Eicher didn't seem too broken up about sitting next to Delia Wagler.

Heading south through Grand Teton, Seth found himself having two conversations—one out loud with Janelle, and an imaginary one with Sharon. Luckily, Janelle spent more time talking to Emily Kuepfer. Poor Carl was doing his best to entertain Beth, but one woman's entertainment was clearly another woman's cross to bear. Sharon would have thought he was hilarious. Finally they just talked about the scenery, which was certainly worth remarking on, but it seemed to Seth that if Carl were trying to get to know Beth, scenery was kind of a low bar.

Finally, he took pity on the poor guy. "Beth, what else have you got in your first-aid kit besides B&W and bandages?"

She glanced at his reflection in the window glass. "It's not very big. A little pair of scissors. Needles in case someone gets a sliver. A little bottle of hydrogen peroxide. A tin of Band-Aid strips. And some fabric I could use either for a sling or to tear in half for a tourniquet."

His stomach did a little twist at this echo of what he'd been thinking last night. "You're thinking someone's going to bleed that bad?"

"Well, the thing about first-aid kits is that you don't know what's going to happen, so you prepare a little and hope a lot that you don't have to use any of it."

Jeannie put in, "This is only the fourth day and look what's already happened—a fall in the river, a burn, and an ambush by a tent."

Carl was the first to laugh.

"Three's a charm—I hope the accidents are all behind us now," Lori called from the front. "How's your hand, Delia?"

"It's better," she said, waggling her bandaged hand. "Beth put some more B&W on it after breakfast."

"If it gets any worse, you tell me, all right? We can find an urgent care clinic if you need it. There's one in Rock Springs."

"I'll be fine," Delia assured her. "It hardly hurts at all."

Jackson Hole lay behind them now, and Seth remembered suddenly that they were in Wyoming, a state he'd never been to before. "Are there any Amish churches in Wyoming?" he asked. "When we lived in New Mexico, we were the last and only. When my dad died and my mother sold the ranch to move to the Siksika, the bishop told us he was only waiting for us to go before he did."

"There are a couple," Catherine said. "But we're going in

the wrong direction for a visit—they're east of Yellowstone, not south."

"Too bad," Tim said. "A good reason for another trip, maybe."

"My dad said that when he first moved there," Seth mused, "one of the first signs he was getting close to New Mexico was the red rocks. Not so much in the Chama River region, but farther south and east."

"You'll get plenty of red rocks at Arches," Lori assured them.

They saw them long before that. They stopped for a picnic lunch beside the Green River where it cut through layers of rock to form Flaming Gorge. The *Youngie* from Pennsylvania couldn't get enough of the sight, taking their sandwiches to walk along the grassy bank, gazing up and up at the brilliant colors—intense red, orange, burnt sienna, brown, even purple in the shadows. Everywhere they looked, the red rocks contrasted with blue sky and dark green pines.

"We're no strangers to red rocks and soil," Emily said. "Remember in *Anne of Green Gables* when Anne asked Matthew why the roads were red?"

"Same reason as here, maybe," Jude mused, drinking it in. "More interesting than the dirt-colored dirt we have, for sure and certain."

"I'm beginning to feel right at home," Seth murmured. It hadn't even been a year since they'd left, but he'd missed the vivid colors of New Mexico. He'd thought Tim was walking beside him, but Beth answered.

"I'm beginning to feel the opposite," she confessed. "I've never seen colors like this. Imagine what Malena could do with a quilt if she saw them."

"You'll have to tell her."

"I don't have words to describe it. Or a phone to take pictures."

"Luckily Carl does. You could ask him to print a few and send them to you."

She huffed a sound that might have been a laugh. "Wouldn't that start a rumor. People would think that we were writing."

That hadn't occurred to him. When a man and a young woman corresponded, it meant they were courting. Separated maybe by distance or finances, but keeping the relationship alive through letters, the way his cousin Adam had written to that girl in Pennsylvania. The wrong sister, it turned out, but now he and the *right* sister, Kate, were completing the home they would move into on the Circle M after they were married in November.

Trust a girl to think that one letter in the mail meant a courtship.

Wait—was she putting the words *Carl* and *courtship* together in her mind? Couldn't she see that she was way too smart for him?

But he doubted Beth would see any such thing. That would show *hochmut*, and no one wanted to be guilty of thinking themselves above another. The very definition of pride.

When lunch was over and the trash disposed of, they were on their way again. But now that the thought of Beth and Carl together had entered his mind, he couldn't shake it. Maybe he'd just keep his eyes open. If the other man came on too strong, she would need someone around to protect her.

❧ 6 ❧
FRIDAY, SEPTEMBER 16

7:00 a.m.

THEY'D ARRIVED at the campground in Moab too late the night before to go hiking, which meant everyone was raring to go early Friday after breakfast. They all piled into the van and, once they used their timed ticket to enter the park, drank in the sight of the rocks and grasses against the deep blue sky of autumn. And Beth marveled at how warm it was already. Like summer.

"I know our start was early," Lori said, "but I want us to see as much as we can before it gets too hot. Girls, you might want to wear scarves instead of your coverings, so you can protect your heads from the sun. And slather some sunscreen on those faces. I don't think Beth has enough of that Burn and Wound stuff to treat all of you for sunburn."

It was eighteen miles around the driving loop, but there was so much to see and marvel at that it took nearly all morning. As they got out to see the Double Arch, Lori had one last warning. "We're at altitude up here, and while the Montana and Colorado folks are used to it, the Pennsylvania folks probably aren't. Take a bottle of water with you, even if it's not far. Dehydration is your enemy."

Beth found the walking pretty easy, though not one of them wore what could be called hiking boots. The young men wore the work boots they'd wear to muck out stalls, except for Carl Yutzy, who wore low-heeled leather boots, scuffed and worn right about where they rubbed against a horse's stirrups. She, like most of the other girls, wore sneakers. All she had at home were snow boots, and they would have taken up too much room. And been unbearably hot on a day where she'd already stuffed her cardigan in her little day pack with the water. But her sneakers had nice thick soles and were well broken in, so she wasn't too afraid of getting blisters.

That would really spoil anybody's plans to hike here in a wilderness that had clearly seen the hand of *Gott* at work.

Double Arch, the signs said. What were the odds of one arch being created here, much less two together? But the price of seeing natural beauty was that you had to walk to find it. Their group began to stretch out as people stopped to look at the landscape. Beth walked steadily on until, like a curtain being pulled back, the two arches came into view.

Her feet slowed to a stop. Her mouth fell open. And it felt as though her soul were rising up to greet these great miracles in stone. To marvel at such massive, soaring structures made of solid rock, and the God Whose hand had carved them.

Lieber Gott, I thank Thee for giving me the opportunity to see what Thou hast created, away out here where for countless centuries the earliest peoples might have stood and marveled just like I am doing now. I thank Thee for making these bridges look as though they might carry a person to Heaven. I thank Thee for bringing me here. Unex-

pected as this trip was, I'm glad Thou didst prompt me to step outside myself, so that Thou canst fill me with wonder.

She came back to herself slowly, feeling utterly at peace yet utterly insignificant in comparison to the massive bridges above her head.

A foot scraped on a rock behind her, and she turned to see Seth Miller, gazing up with his mouth open just as hers had been. The Double Arch was probably used to that. It was their due, she thought whimsically.

Seth's eyes closed, and she realized he hadn't even seen her. And that he was speaking to *der Herr* in just the same way. For the first time, she got a glimpse of his inner life, his spiritual service to the One they both worshipped, instead of merely seeing the laconic young man who lobbed remarks at people to see if they'd react. Who didn't seem to have thought about a path for his life, yet from all accounts was very good at what he did on the Circle M for his uncle.

Seth Miller was a puzzle. She had seen him at what she'd thought was his best, hauling her out of the river and saving her life. But now she wondered if this moment was the best of him, speaking to his Father out of the depths of his soul.

Just as she had a minute ago. Had he seen her the way she was seeing him now?

A week ago, she'd have shuddered at the thought of his seeing what was meant to be private. But now? Now it felt more like an experience they shared.

Yes, shared. If he even realized it was her standing here, and not one of the others.

She stood motionless, the wind tugging at her skirts and her *Duchly*. When his eyes opened, she still didn't move. He was looking up, just as she had been.

And then he said, as though picking up a conversation

they'd begun earlier, "They're like a physical version of *Gottes wille*, aren't they?"

Who was he talking to? She glanced behind him, but the others hadn't joined them yet. *Ja*, he was talking to her. "I was just thinking that. Thanking Him for a path as solid as those arches, carrying us up and up to *Himmel*."

"On a *very* strait and narrow way." The corners of his mouth tipped up in a smile. "Though you probably wouldn't survive if you left that path up there before your journey was done."

Together, they gazed up, following the massive curves. "Look," she said, pointing. "They really are joined at the bottom. Imagine creating something like that."

"The folks at the visitors' center say it was sand and wind."

"I don't doubt it was. But Someone created that sand, and directed the wind."

"And God saw that it was good," he quoted.

A shout came from behind them, and the others straggled over the crest and into the saddle of rock where they were standing. Beth felt the moment of communion dissolve, even though several of their companions had also felt the magnificence of the Double Arch, and were gazing awestruck at the reddish stone. Perhaps they were having a moment of worship themselves.

But she held her moment close to her heart—those seconds of feeling at one with her Creator in worship of His handiwork.

At one—in a way—with Seth. Which was both comforting and unsettling.

After everyone had had their fill of the wonder of the Double Arch, they walked back down to the van for the picnic lunch the breakfast partners had prepared. Egg salad sandwiches and quartered apples tasted pretty good in the warm sunshine, sitting on a rock by the side of the loop road. They washed them down with water, and then Lori produced chocolate bars from the cooler for dessert.

Seth took two chocolate bars and walked over to offer Delia one. *"Neh, denki,"* she said. "I'm allergic to chocolate."

His face took on a pained expression while Emily and Beth groaned in sympathy.

"It's my cross to bear," Delia said with a tip of her head and a lift of one shoulder. "I try to look on the bright side—it could have been wheat products. I do love my bread … and cake … and pasta of every possible shape." Ruefully, she patted her stomach in a way that acknowledged her curvy figure had probably had help from everything on that list.

Seth turned and held out the chocolate bar to Beth, who was sitting close by enjoying her warm chunk of rock with its flat top. "You're not allergic, are you?"

She shook her head and took it, squashing the tiny pang of disappointment that he hadn't offered it to her first. But why should he? One moment of wonder did not mean that he now found her as interesting as Delia. Some girls just had that gift. Sharon Keim, for instance. And Malena Miller. Malena's sister Rebecca was like Beth herself—quiet and invisible and easily overlooked. But one man had been led to Rebecca by *Gott*. Noah King had *seen* her, really seen her, and that made all the difference.

What right did Beth have to be anyone's first choice? How *hochmut* was that? Even her father, who was supposed to love his children second only to God and his wife, hadn't seen her except when she did something wrong. It was too much to expect that she could compete with the likes of Delia and Sharon.

Then she shook her head at herself. It was too beautiful a day to be down in the dumps about a silly little disappointment she had no right to. She had no interest in competition of any kind. Nor did she want that kind of attention from Seth Miller. He was her brother in the Lord, that was all.

They all climbed back into the van and drove to the trailhead for Landscape Arch. "We'd go to Delicate Arch—the one you see on all the calendars—but at this time of day it's too hot and too vertical," Lori said. "Landscape Arch is about a mile out and the same back, mostly level. A bit more doable for our Eastern friends."

Even Beth, who had lived at the Siksika Valley altitude for several years now, was feeling it. And while the sun was pleasantly warm, she definitely felt the need for another coat of sunscreen in the thinner air.

When she got her first look at Landscape Arch, she couldn't help but frown. "A formation as pretty as that needs a better name," she said to Carl Yutzy, who happened to walk up right then, and stood next to her taking it in.

"What would you call it if you were the explorer who discovered it?"

"I expect it had a name before any explorer got here," she said wryly. "Like they said at the visitors' center. But if it was up to me, I'd call it something like Seeing Eye Arch."

"Like a seeing eye dog?" He chuckled.

"No, more like what you see through that opening is unique. You only get a narrow view, but if you have eyes to see, it's marvelous."

"Marvel Arch," he suggested. "Isn't there a Marble Arch somewhere? This is just rock."

"Sandstone."

"Which is a rock."

She wasn't about to argue, since she could barely tell sandstone from slate herself. It wasn't like they'd learned desert geology in the little one-room schoolhouse back in Whinburg Township. Everything she knew had come from the displays at the visitors' center.

"What did you think of Double Arch?" she asked instead.

"Pretty big. I wouldn't want to be under it when pieces flake off."

The signs on the trail here warned that hikers could no longer go right under Landscape Arch for just that reason.

"Neither would I. But how did it make you feel?"

He glanced at her curiously. "Feel? Small, I guess. That thing was huge. Both of them. Why, how did you feel?"

"Like I was looking at *Gottes wille* in solid form—a bridge to heaven."

His sandy brows went up and he tipped his felt hat back a little with one finger, exposing a band of sweating skin and darkened blond hair. "You don't talk much, but when you do, you don't mess around."

She wasn't sure if this was a compliment from a man who could look at the Double Arch and merely observe that it was big.

She shrugged. "It's just how I felt."

"What about its name? What would you change it to? Twin Bridges?"

"That sounds like something you'd find in a city. Neh, I might call it Twin Windows. You see differently, don't you, after you look through them."

"Well, evidently you did. Are you always this poetic?"

There was a first time for everything—like being called *poetic*. Maybe he really was trying to give her a compliment.

Which was a first in itself. She'd never had a compliment from someone she wasn't closely related to.

"I don't think so," she admitted with a smile. "But there's something about this canyon country that's out of the ordinary. Maybe it deserves a little poetry."

"If Cora Swarey was here, she'd have already written a hymn," he mused. "Probably about bridges to heaven and ... those other things you said."

"Do you know her? You're from Amity, too, aren't you? We love getting copies of her hymns, and singing them on Sunday nights."

"We're in the same church district. You heard she's getting married early next year?"

"I heard." Cora's intended, Simon Yoder, was from Whinburg Township, and Mamm had news from there regularly.

"It's too bad," Carl said sadly. "I was sweet on her for a while. But there was no getting her attention once she met Simon. I might as well have been invisible."

Beth could have made some remark about God deciding which man was right for which woman. Instead, she turned to gaze at the view through the arch and tried not to think about feeling invisible.

What would Seth have named this formation?

"Say, Beth, we're only staying the one night here. Why don't we sit together tomorrow for the road to Canyonlands? You're more interesting to talk to than my sister."

Her first instinct was to put him off—say that it was hard to predict where a person would sit when everyone was trying to get into the van at once. But Seth was standing just on the edge of earshot, and something about the stillness of his pose made her wonder if he was listening. Not that it mattered—it wasn't like she and Carl were having a *moment*.

Still. This was why she'd come, wasn't it? To see things she'd never seen before, and do things she'd never done?

"Sure," she said, before she could reason herself out of it. "That would be fun."

Saturday, September 17

After supper the night before (chili dogs covered in chopped onion and melted cheese, courtesy of Tim Eicher and Janelle Stutzman, with potato chips and store-bought cake for dessert), the group had decided that on the next day they wanted to see, in Delia's words, "Something we'll always remember."

Lori had grinned and allowed that there were a couple of places on their route where she might be able to arrange that. But, she warned, it would mean getting up and having breakfast while it was still dark. Not one of them was a stranger to getting up in the dark—the work day on the Circle M often began at four a.m. and ended at eight o'clock in the evening. So that morning, they'd eaten their bacon and eggs by lantern light and tried to be as quiet as possible as they broke camp, so as not to disturb the sleeping *Englisch* in the sites closest to them.

Seth had wondered if Carl Yutzy meant to go through with his plan to sit with Beth. It took some courage to just come right out and suggest it, especially with people around. But would he go through with it, or pretend he'd forgotten?

But *neh*, there he was, holding the van door and ushering her inside to the row of three and offering her the window seat to boot. Not that there was anything to see yet except a vague silhouette of rock spires against a sky that was still thinking about whether or not dawn was an option.

"Denki," Seth heard her say as he approached the door. "I like this seat. It's just right for seeing everything."

Carl took the middle one and some impulse had Seth climbing in. "Mind if I join you?" he asked, and parked his long body on Carl's other side.

So much for the two of them getting in any private conversation. Strange how he felt no regret. There was no time for that anyway, because the others were piling in after him, with Chris bringing up the rear and claiming the single seat. Seth would have some competition for space to stretch his legs.

"What are we going to see, Lori?" Jeannie asked from beside her.

"It's called Mesa Arch, and that's all I'm going to say about it. I just hope we'll get there in time, and if we do, that we don't have fifty people for company."

"Well, that clears things up," Carl said cheerfully.

"It can't be far away if she means to get there for sunrise," Beth ventured. "Do you suppose that's it?"

"I hope not," he replied. "Maybe it's somewhere on the way south. You'll have just enough time to tell me about yourself."

It was all Seth could do to control his impulse to turn and gape at the guy. This was the most forward Carl had been since the van had rolled into the yard at the Circle M. He hadn't known he had it in him.

Beth's voice was almost as surprised. "Me? You already know. We all went around the circle that first night, remember? Or were you asleep?"

"That wasn't getting to know anybody. That was making sure we weren't related to each other. In case we wanted to … you know."

"Hook up?" Seth supplied, gazing past Chris out the window and sounding crude on purpose.

Beth took the bait with a snap. "I hate that expression. It's too *Englisch*. It makes people sound like clothing fasteners."

Carl laughed. "Or a gate. Stay away from the guy who's like a piston latch. You'll never get away."

Had Beth been around cowboys long enough to know what a piston latch was? Probably.

"Is that why you're on this trip, Carl?" Seth asked idly, as though the answer didn't matter much to him. Just passing time as the darkness slid by. Nothing to see here.

Seth felt Carl's shoulders rise and fall in a shrug. "Isn't that why any of us are here? Maybe a little for the scenery. And just to travel. To get away from the same old hills and cows for a couple of weeks. Definitely not as many cows here."

"No grass," Beth pointed out.

"Exactly. That's different. Those arches yesterday were different. I wonder how many Amish folk have seen them."

There was no answering that. Except— "Eleven for sure, I guess."

He laughed again. "Besides us, I meant."

"I'm on this trip for the adventure," she said suddenly.

Another surprise. But Seth had to admit it was a better reason than getting away from cows. "You've had your share already," he said to her. "Though I suppose you could have fallen in the Siksika River for that kind of adventure, and saved yourself the drive."

"I'm fine with the Madison River being the one and only time," she said fervently. "It was definitely an adventure I'll pass on next time."

"But you had a strong hero to rescue you," said Delia from behind her. "He saved your life. That's my kind of adventure."

Was the whole van listening? Whose idea was it to cast him

like the brawny guys on the covers of the romance novels in the Bell, Book and Candle bookshop in Mountain Home?

"I'm not sure Seth would see it that way," Beth mumbled.

"But what a great story to tell your grandchildren," Tim piped up. He'd snagged the seat next to Delia, which hadn't amused Seth one bit.

"Whose grandchildren?" he demanded.

"Yours and Beth's, of course." There was just enough light now to see Tim's white teeth. "Seth and Beth. You guys were made for each other, with names like that."

What had got into him? "See if I pull *you* out of any rivers, *freind*," he said, keeping his voice level. "Or even a dry arroyo. With a hungry mountain lion in the bottom."

Carl laughed, and Delia seemed to appreciate his attempt at cowboy humor.

"I for one hope you find your adventure," Emily said, reaching forward to touch Beth's shoulder and bring the conversation back to her, where it belonged. "That's partly why I came, too. Though I guess it won't be a rescue from drowning, since I can swim. I wonder what mine will be?"

"Not running into M—" Janelle stopped abruptly.

An expectant silence fell as everyone waited for her to finish. A diesel rig passed them with a roar.

"Into *mmm*—what?" Jude prompted her.

"Nothing," Emily said.

"Come on, Janelle, that sounded interesting," he persisted. "Emily's adventure would be not running into what?"

"Mountain lions," Beth said suddenly. "Tim, remember those hikers in the state park in the valley? They walked around a rockfall and there he was, nine feet long from whiskers to tail, standing in the path."

"There's an adventure I'd pass on," Tim said. "You can't

run, because the prey instinct will kick in and the cat will chase you. All you can do is make a lot of noise and pretend to be bigger than it is."

"Is that what they did?" Delia's pretty eyes were wide.

"They had on yellow ponchos because it was raining, so they waved their arms and hollered," Seth remembered aloud. "I read it in the paper."

Tim went on, "It wasn't until they got down to the parking lot that they remembered they had an air horn in one of the backpacks just for that purpose. They were so scared they never even thought of it."

The conversation ended abruptly as Lori made the turn into Canyonlands. "That was it for today's drive?" Carl complained. "How's a man to get to know someone in only half an hour?"

"I'm sure you'll find a way," Lori said once they were through the entrance gate. "But right now we're heading for Island in the Sky."

Beth sat up straight. "Really? What is that? It sounds wonderful."

"It's the area we're going to."

"Island in the Sky," she repeated, her voice filled with delight. "If that isn't the perfect place for an adventure, I don't know what is."

❦　7　❦

THE HIKE along the trail up to Mesa Arch was barely thirty minutes in the dim grey of dawn. Lori had been hurrying them, so Tim walked close to Delia to help her along, though it wasn't steep, just a bit rocky. Except for themselves, the trail was deserted, which Seth considered a *gut* thing.

For some annoying reason, Carl was stuck to Beth like glue. Was this where it started? Far enough from home and everything familiar that they could get on with pairing up? Weren't they supposed to be enjoying God's creation and looking for adventure?

Seth was beginning to feel slightly annoyed at his friend Tim as well. It wasn't like Seth could pursue Emily—they were cousins, for Pete's sake. Janelle was too fluttery and always at Emily's side, as though she were afraid to have an adventure of her own. Catherine ... well, he didn't know her at all. She just giggled when her brother made a joke, and gazed longingly at Jude, who seemed completely oblivious.

Beth was the only one he wasn't related to who seemed to be ... well, interesting. Not what he'd thought she was. She was still aloof and quiet, though she was opening up a little. But he couldn't forget that moment at Double Arch when animosity had been left behind. In that few seconds of peace and accord in the shared experience of spontaneous worship, he had suddenly understood what the scriptures meant about Ananias.

And immediately there fell from his eyes as it had been scales: and he received sight forthwith...

Not physical sight. Seth's blindness, he had just begun to understand, was the inside kind. The kind that came from his habit of keeping people at a distance—and not only people. Jobs. A future. He held people off just enough to be neighborly, but too far away to *see* them. Even Tim, whom he considered his closest friend outside his immediate family, didn't know his innermost thoughts and feelings. For that matter, neither did his own brothers. Seth knew plenty about theirs, and as for Tim, it never occurred to him that he wouldn't be as interesting to others as they were to him.

But for the first time, Seth realized that friendship wasn't just about exchanging stories or observations on the harvest or predictions about the cattle market. It was about seeing who a person was. And allowing them to see you.

Maybe Tim had something that Seth didn't. Maybe, he thought as the group reached the top of the trail and thirty feet of arch rose out of the stone to greet them, he had been managing his life the wrong way. Maybe it was already too late to fix it, at least when it came to a woman like—

The sun crested the mesas to the east, and light flooded through the aperture of the arch. Seth sucked in his breath as the rocks caught fire, the light illuminating both the arch and the stone beneath it so that the pink and orange glow reflected from one to the other. Solid stone almost looked translucent, the way a finger did when you held it up in front of a flame.

Beth gasped, her eyes wide in awe. Seth was so arrested by the sight of her, cheeks warmed by the reflection of light, that it was a few seconds before he realized he was staring at her, not the arch. Behind her were two *Englisch* photographers bent to massive cameras on tripods, clicking so fast it sounded like a pair of cicadas.

The light was already changing, its intensity moving from the bottom of the arch to the middle, striking beams of brilliance on their little group where they'd been in the blue and purple shade a second before, turning the buff-colored rocks red and orange.

Let there be light, and there was light.

Without the photographers, with only themselves as witness, it would have felt like that first day.

Beth turned, and their wide eyes met. He could almost hear her thinking. *Isn't this wunderbaar? Isn't it a miracle?*

All he could do was nod. He might even have smiled. Because her hazel eyes sparkled in the rosy light and she smiled back, as though they were completely alone.

"Wow," Carl Yutzy said, stepping into the sun's beam and casting her in shadow. "Would you look at that."

Seth came crunching back to earth, his boot turning on a stone and making him stagger. By the time he got control of his feet, the light had changed yet again, the arch blocking the body of the sun but making the entire sky glow white above and below it.

"Bischt du okay?" his cousin Emily murmured. "You don't want to turn an ankle up here."

"Ja, I'm okay." He cracked open the vault of his reserve enough to admit, "Just ... a little overwhelmed by all this."

"Me too," she said softly, with no reserve at all, looking away as the sun peeked over the arch and lit up yet another outcropping of rocks behind them. Better to look at the effect of the light rather than the light itself. "The red rocks at home are pretty at sunset, but it's nothing like this."

Beth joined them, almost hesitantly, as though if she looked away from the arch she might miss something. "If the sound of Gabriel's trumpet were light," she said softly, "it would have been like that. Like a shout of triumph made of sunrise."

Before he could stop himself, he said, "Every sunrise is like that. Even the wet, snowy ones when I'm looking for calves in February. The triumph of light over darkness."

She tilted her head so that once again, their eyes met. "Exactly. Some places have forgotten it. Like cities, maybe. But this place ... it will never forget."

And wasn't that something to thank *der Herr* for?

"That was *wunderbaar*—I mean, amazing," Catherine said to Lori. "Thank you for bringing us here."

Their driver's face held a quiet satisfaction now that she'd shepherded her flock safely up to the sunrise in time. "I thought it was pretty *wunderbaar*, too," she said, her pronunciation of the word surprisingly good. "Those photographers—I think they did as well, in their own way. But I've had one or two groups up here..." She shook her head, and her short greyish-blond curls bounced. "They were more interested in taking selfies to prove they were here than to actually experience *being* here." Her keen blue eyes behind her glasses glanced off Seth, then Beth, who was gazing at the sky ripening to blue in the aperture of the arch. "I was watching some of you. You *appreciated* it. That makes all the driving worthwhile."

They spent the next half hour or so exploring under the

arch and up into the rocks. Jude even gathered the courage to walk right up to the arch and lay a hand on it, gently, as if it were a sleeping animal. Catherine clasped her hands as though she expected something terrible to happen ... until he waved her up beside him.

When the sun had climbed enough to flatten the light into normalcy, Chris and Jeannie rounded them up and they headed back down the trail. Their next stop was Aztec Butte, which was not a gentle half hour's walk. It was more like an hour of rocks and stairs and some scrambling, and Delia was red-faced by the time she reached the gathering point. Seth had to give her credit, though. Not a word of complaint crossed her lips, and when she stopped to rest, she was the one who spotted the crumbling adobe structure tucked under an overhang of slick sandstone.

"Is this a house?" Catherine peered into its small square opening, which wouldn't have admitted anything taller than a child.

"No, a granary," Lori said. "The Pueblo people's equivalent of a root cellar. They would store food and supplies here. This must have been a popular spot, because there are several of them. You're welcome to look around for the others, but don't go climbing into one. Some of them are a thousand years old."

A thousand years. Seth could hardly imagine it.

"Wish I was a good enough buggy maker that my work would last a thousand years," Chris Kauffman joked.

"I'm pretty sure there would have been someone around to fix things up every century or so, when the bricks began to weather." Seth knelt beside the little structure that only came up to his waist, and dared to touch one of the cool, crumbling adobe bricks with a single finger.

"The stories it could tell," Beth murmured, standing just behind his shoulder. "It even *smells* old here."

"I never thought I'd see something a human being made a thousand years ago, just standing out here in the wind and weather, not in a museum. Especially not in North America. In the old country, my *grossdaadi* used to say, there were *Englisch* cathedrals that old, but even he had never seen one. Only pictures."

"I didn't know anything like this existed. I wonder how—"

Someone shouted from around the curve of the trail, and Seth rose and dusted off his pants. "Come on. Maybe they found another."

They had—and then some.

"Oh, my goodness," Beth breathed as the earth fell away beneath their stunned gazes and they looked out across miles of mesas and buttes and canyons, red and ochre and buff, deepening to purple and blue on the horizon.

"Wow," Carl said for the second time. "Now, that's a view."

The wind tugged at the girls' headscarves and made their skirts flap. Seth felt the push of it on his chest. "We might be the first obstruction this wind has seen since it left California."

One thing about this trip—it was certainly giving him a new appreciation for God's creation. At one time, the thought of California would have filled him with frustrated longing. He'd be up here looking west and wishing he could grow wings and fly, to see things none of his family had seen, to do things they'd never thought of doing. But instead he was standing up here on this overlook, feeling small and insignificant ... and realizing that wasn't so bad. His imagination might have wings, but his body sure didn't. He couldn't even climb into those canyons down there, looking like ditches from this height. And he certainly couldn't get out again.

"Man has his place," he murmured, aware that Beth was standing nearby. Then again, so were at least half the group. "But I don't think he and his inventions are welcome in some of those canyons."

"True enough," Lori responded over her shoulder. "But I know a way down into one of them, if you'd like to get up close and personal. A little off the beaten track, but doable for this group. Some of you are related to mountain goats, I think."

Seth wasn't sure that was a compliment—in the Bible, goats were people who weren't willing for the guidance of the Shepherd, and were separated out of the flock. But no, she couldn't have meant that. He had to admit that with certain people, like Jude, there was a definite resemblance to the exploratory habits of mountain goats.

"We might be in for some weather." Emily pointed off to the north. "Those clouds look so strange, don't they? Like they're walking."

Instead of piling up together like the ones in Montana, here as in New Mexico, the clouds seemed to separate. Far away in the distance, Seth could see silvery skeins of rain trailing behind them as they drifted across the landscape.

"At least you can tell where they're going," Chris said. "I suppose it would give you lots of time to get out of the way."

"They're like this where I grew up, too," Seth told them. "I remember Mamm making my *dat* pull up the horses while a cloud dumping rain crossed the road in front of us on the way to church. She didn't want us to get there soaking wet in our open buggy."

Beth smiled at the picture he painted, and a little glow of pleasure ignited inside him. She had a great smile. She didn't show it very often, which made it all the more surprising when it flashed at some unexpected joke or observation.

"All right, then. We'll look around a bit here, then on the way south we'll stop at Náshdóítsoh Canyon and do a little exploring around," Lori said, turning reluctantly from the view. "There's a dry riverbed in the bottom, but the big thing about it is there are some petroglyphs there. It's on tribal land, not in the national park, so not too many people know about them."

"What was that word you said?" Jeannie was the keeper of the map, following their route with it on her lap. Clearly it wasn't familiar.

"Náshdóítsoh. It's a Navajo word. Means *mountain lion*."

Nash dough eat so. Seth repeated it in his head. "Hope we don't meet any of those."

"I'll do my best to keep them off the itinerary," Lori said with a grin. "Some of these rifts and canyons have names that don't show up on the maps. I visit a Navajo friend every time I come out this way, and that's what she calls it. We'll be seeing her family a little farther along the route."

They found two more of the little ruins that had been granaries, and then Chris declared it was time for lunch. They hiked back down to where the van was parked, and if he hadn't been hungry before, Seth certainly was after the forty-five-minute walk. They owed today's lunch to Catherine and Jude, which arrangement Seth was pretty certain had been engineered by a conspiracy of girls. The sliced turkey, ham, and Swiss cheese from the deli in Moab tasted *gut* on Kaiser rolls, though, with bean sprouts heaped up and lots of mayo and mustard slathered on.

"These pickles taste almost as good as Willard Zook's," Beth said around a bite of sandwich and crunchy pickle. "I hope I can convince him to give me his recipe some day."

"Is he really going to marry your mother?" Tim asked. "He's

been around my whole life. I always think of him as ancient. And your mamm is only forty something, right?"

"She was forty-five in July. And Will isn't ancient. He's not even sixty." Beth leaped to his defense like a kitten to that of a cattle dog. "He's kind and talented and he adores her. If a man looked at me that way—" She stopped and took another bite of her sandwich, but Seth didn't miss the sudden flush in her cheeks.

"You'd what?" Tim teased. "Ask him for his recipes?"

She tilted her chin at him. "I'd be happy, that's what. Not that *you'd* know anything about it."

"What, making you happy?" Tim laughed, but a flush was rising under his own cheekbones. Because he didn't want anyone to think of him and Beth that way? Or because he secretly thought that way himself?

Seth swallowed his bite of sandwich hard.

"No, the things Willard does that make a woman happy." Now her color seemed less from embarrassment than irritation. "Putting Mamm first, for instance. Do you do that, Tim?"

"Now, now..." Jeannie began.

Tim looked as though a tiny firecracker had gone off under his nose. "I didn't mean—"

"I won't have a word said against Willard Zook." Beth's eyes snapped. "Whether he marries my mother or not, he's our family's friend."

Seth stared at her. This was literally the first time he'd ever seen Beth Stolzfus angry. He hadn't realized that was even possible. And in defense of Willard Zook, of all people.

"I'm sorry, Beth," Tim said, his face aflame. "You're right. He's our brother, and I'm ashamed now of all the times I made fun of him."

Beth seemed to simmer down, like a kettle once the flame

has been turned off. "And I'm sorry I lost my temper. Will has been *gut* to us. I wish everyone could see his fine qualities and appreciate him like we do. His brother Hezekiah, too."

"So how is that going to work if your *mamm* marries him?" Seth asked. "Has she talked about it with you?"

"I think they're still working that out," Beth admitted. "But if anyone asked me, I'd say we should all move to the Zook place. Mamm wouldn't have to pay rent on the house as well as the quilt shop, and goodness knows there's enough room over there. The Zooks were a big family."

"After Calvin risked his life to help with the renovations to your house, too," Tim said, shaking his head sadly.

Beth made a rude noise. "Calvin Yoder risks his life every day simply by existing. As for the renovations, we've enjoyed them. And so will the next family his dad rents to. If it comes to that."

"Maybe it will be us," Chris Kauffman said suddenly.

The entire group turned to stare at him. Including his wife.

Now it was his turn to blush. "Sorry, *Liebling*," he said to Jeannie. "But we have been talking about moving away from Pennsylvania."

"I didn't think you meant *this* far away." Her voice was a little higher than usual.

"But they need a buggy maker in the west, and there are already three within twenty miles of Whinburg. I've been wanting to go out on my own," he said to the group at large. Then his gaze locked with Jeannie's. "I'd never do anything without talking it over with you, you know that. But if *der Herr* prompts us..."

Jeannie nibbled her lips and her lashes fell. "F-A-I-T-H."

They all knew what that meant. So when Lori suddenly

said, *"Forsaking all, I trust Him,"* Seth nearly fell off the rock he was sitting on.

Without thinking, they had all been speaking *Deitsch*. That last part had been in *Englisch*, but still.

Lori looked up from her lunch, the color seeping into her cheeks now. "I've been keeping a little something from you," she said slowly. "I didn't mean to, because you've all mostly been speaking English and it didn't come up. But as a child, I spent all my summers in Wisconsin with my Amish grandparents. I've been speaking *Deitsch* since I was six."

"Your family is Amish?" Janelle said in amazement.

"My parents left the church when my brother was born. I don't know why," Lori confessed. "All I know is that I didn't see my grandparents until I went to stay with them that first summer. And met more cousins and aunts and uncles than I knew what to do with. I've kept it up, driving for the Amish." She paused. "I didn't mean to deceive you all."

"Of course you didn't," Seth said, when surprise seemed to be silencing everyone else. "I guess we'll have to mind what we say in both languages now."

When Lori laughed, a chuckle of relief went around the group. "I guess you'd sure better. So, has everyone finished their lunch? We need to get on the road if we want to see the petroglyphs while the light is good."

❧ 8 ☙

Náshdóítsoh Canyon wasn't marked; you couldn't even see it during the hour's walk from where the van was parked. Lori had made sure they were well supplied with water and snacks. Then, just when Beth was wondering of the trail would ever end, or if they'd have to spend the night on the mesa, they came to a cliff that plunged into a narrow canyon, its sandstone walls striped in layers of red and brown.

Like a row of little sheep, they followed her past a hand-scrawled sign nailed to a fence post.

Danger Steep
Floods

Beth took a deep breath. Lori would never bring them to a place that was actually dangerous, would she? No, of course not. She was twice as old as any of them, so if she could do it, so could they. As for floods, maybe in Noah's time, but certainly not now.

The trail was narrow but not difficult to navigate, and

zigzagged down the canyon wall following what looked like an ancient creek bed. There was only one really steep section of what Lori called *slickrock*, but someone hundreds of years ago had chipped out handholds in it, just big enough to hold a person's toes in a running shoe.

When Beth reached the bottom, Seth and Tim reached up to make sure her last jump to the ground was as easy as possible. After that, the trail took a shallower, more comfortable course all the way to the creek bed, where green tussocks of some hardy grass and golden clumps of rabbit bush hinted that there was water close by, even if the sandy soil looked dry.

"The petroglyphs are upstream just a little way," Lori said. "A few hundred yards at most. Everyone feel like going on?"

"I think I'll just stay here and explore around a bit," Delia said. "It's pretty, and I want to save my energy for the climb back up."

"I'll stay with you," Catherine said at once.

"I guess I'd better stay, too. You know, to protect you from the mountain lions," Jude said with a grin.

Beth resisted the urge to roll her eyes. She had a feeling that Jude didn't care for heights, and was regretting coming down here with them all. Mind you, that climb down the slickrock hadn't been easy for anyone. But he'd stayed well back at the lookout at Aztec Butte, too, and had been more interested in the granaries than in any view. Which was fine. She could empathize. Beth didn't mind heights, but she still hadn't recovered from that terrifying few minutes in the Madison River. The fact that this canyon didn't have so much as a trickle in the bottom was a definite plus.

Jeannie and Chris decided to stay behind, too, and enjoy the sun and the warmth while the others went on. That left only six following Lori along the sandy bottom of the canyon.

"This is the easiest walking we've had all day," Emily observed with a smile of relief.

"Our reward for that climb down the slickrock," Janelle said. "At least going back up will be easier. We'll be able to see better where the footholds are."

Lori pointed to a stand of what looked like poplars in a sunny patch against the cliff. Their leaves had already turned gold and Beth drank in the beautiful sight against the red sandstone. They made their way over and slipped between the trunks.

"Here," Lori said, pointing to the ancient markings on the stone. "Don't touch them. The oil on our fingers can damage them."

"Seems funny that something you don't even think about can damage them, when they've been here for how many hundreds of years, in all kinds of weather." Seth squatted to get a better look. "This one is a spiral. The sun, maybe?"

"No, that one there is the sun." Beth pointed to a circle surrounded by short rays, chipped out of the rock by something harder than sandstone. "I should have paid better attention at the visitors' center in the park. I know one of the rangers was talking about spirals."

"Do you suppose this is an antelope?" Emily squinted at another a few yards away, a brown shape on deeply varnished rock that you would walk right past if you didn't know it was there. The little figure was more of a rectangle with lines sticking out of it, but the twin curves on one end did suggest horns or antlers.

"Could be a deer," Carl said. "Depending on their habitat. Antelopes tend to like wide open spaces, but maybe they were used to canyon country a thousand years ago."

The hand prints were easier to interpret. "I can't help but

think of the handprint turkeys we used to make in school before Thanksgiving," Seth said with a laugh. "Maybe this is a flock of turkeys, telling people the hunting is good here."

"Or identifying a particular human family," Lori mused. "If they're painted, they're called pictographs. These carved ones are the petroglyphs."

"I think the people were just having fun with dyes they made," Janelle said. "Look, here's another spiral. And if that isn't a rabbit, I don't know what is."

"Definitely a rabbit," Beth agreed. "Imagine—a thousand years or more separate us from these ancient people, and I bet there are still rabbits down here."

"That's rabbits for you," Tim said wryly. "Even time can't get rid of them."

"I wish I knew how to draw like your cousin Zach," Beth said wistfully to Seth. "His pictures look so real. Then I'd have something to remember this place by."

"I think we'll remember it," he said softly. "Even if we don't know what some of this means, we know that sometime in the past there was a man like Zach, who couldn't help but draw something important to him. And all these years later, he's still sending that message."

Beth smiled at the thought, and somehow her gaze caught on his the way a skirt catches on a thistle, and it was a second before she could untangle herself from it. And then of course the heat prickled into her cheeks. She could only be grateful that everyone else was spreading along the rocky wall of the canyon looking for more petroglyphs, and not watching her behaving like a *Narr* just because Seth Miller looked at her.

He had nice eyes, though. Brown, with long lashes that had probably got him teased in school. She'd never really looked into them until this trip—she'd always been too busy avoiding his gaze or anybody else's, in case they *saw* her. Which in her experience often meant catching her doing something wrong. Thinking to themselves, *There goes Beth Stolzfus. The one who probably isn't good enough to sing with. To eat with. To date.*

But this trip? She'd been almost shockingly outspoken earlier on Willard's behalf, and not one person seemed to think she was doing anything wrong. On the contrary, Tim Eicher had apologized, right there in front of everybody. And Seth had nodded at what she'd said and come to her support. Well, she'd wanted new experiences, hadn't she? The *gut Gott* was certainly seeing that she got some.

It was warm in the sun, so she left the petroglyphs and wandered across the canyon floor to where the opposite cliff cast a deep shadow. It was lovely and cool, and almost made the colors of stone and plants brighter now that she didn't have to squint to see them.

Seth had followed, and was gazing up at the canyon wall as if he were looking for more ancient markings.

"You boys are lucky to wear hats," she said diffidently, in case he thought she was taking that moment of gazing into each other's eyes as permission to be forward with him. "Even with the sunscreen, my nose is getting sunburned."

"Mine is, too." He chuckled. "I think it's all this looking up. Arches, canyons, birds, sky—I'm always looking up and the sun finds its way under the brim."

"It's like that proverb Willard quotes. *If your eyes are on the earth, you won't see the Son.* But the earth here is pretty interesting." As if to illustrate her point, she took in the sandy creek bed. It looked darker here in the shade, down the middle where the creek might once have run. Quite a lot darker. That was odd. "Seth? Come look at this."

He loped over to join her. "Did you find a fossil?"

"*Neh*, just something strange. No wonder there are so many plants growing here. The water table must be close to the surface—it looks almost wet."

He prodded the sandy dirt with a finger. When he showed her, his fingertip was coated with clinging sand. "It *is* wet. Maybe it had some rain."

"Not here. We've been in this neighborhood for a couple of days and had nothing but sunshine."

"It was raining north of here. It—" He stopped. Bent down. "This *is* strange."

The sand was even darker, glistening as though it was saturated. Even as she watched, water seemed to be filling little channels in the sand.

Lori emerged from the copse of poplars, but none of the others were in sight. Beth called, "Lori, come here a minute?"

By the time she joined them, the tiny rivulets had become a trickle and had overflowed the little channels to become a single runnel.

Lori took one look and sucked in a breath. "*Gott in Himmel.* I should have known when I saw that rain from the overlook. Where are the others?"

Seth shook his head, clearly not understanding her. "I thought they were still with you. They must have gone upstream. No one has passed us in the last couple of minutes."

"Go get them. Now."

Without another word, he set off up the creek bed at a jog.

Beth could hear the *plash* of his boot soles in the water. A chill arrowed through her stomach. "Lori—what is it?"

"Flash flood," she said grimly. "Like the sign said. We can't risk it—we all need to get to higher ground, fast."

Flash flood? But those were only real in the Louis L'Amour

novels one of the old folks in Whinburg used to read. "Higher ground? What will happen?"

"Maybe nothing. Or maybe ten feet of water will get compressed coming down that canyon and carry us all away."

Voices, high and rapid, preceded three figures, running at top speed around a rocky curve and heading for the copse of poplars.

"This way!" Lori shouted. "Back to the trail, and climb like your life depends on it."

She was not exaggerating.

"Where is Emily?" Beth screamed at Janelle, who brought up the rear.

"She went on ahead," Janelle gasped. "Seth went to get her."

Lori was already running after the little group, toward the trail. "Beth, come on!" she shouted over one shoulder.

For a split second, Beth saw herself running away, and leaving Seth and Emily here to face who knew what. If Emily hadn't come back with the others, could she have slipped and hurt herself? What if she needed one of the bandages Beth had in her first-aid kit, bumping along with two bottles of water in her day pack?

Every feeling inside her urged her not to leave, but to go and help.

"Right behind you!" she shrieked at Lori, and took off after Seth.

Lori screamed something, and a lifelong habit of obedience nearly made Beth check her headlong flight and turn back. But she couldn't. Lori needed to get the others up that slickrock, out of reach of the water. And Beth needed to make sure Emily was all right. Needed to make sure Seth got out of here safely. To see with her own eyes that he did.

Narr. He's perfectly capable of looking after himself. He's the one who saves injured cows out there on the mountain. Who delivers calves in a howling blizzard. All you're doing is making twice as much work for him and putting him in danger.

But something told her to go. A little ball of urgency right under her breastbone told her to stop wasting time on second thoughts.

So run she did, dodging rocks and keeping to the smooth sand until she couldn't anymore. Until the water in the channel threatened to soak her sneakers.

"Beth!"

The shout came from a huge cluster of red rocks that had clearly fallen hundreds of feet from the cliff above to make a big barrier across half the canyon.

"What are you doing here?" Seth shouted. "Go back with the others—I'll handle this."

Handle what? Oh goodness, Emily really was hurt!

She poured on the speed and reached the rocks, where she scrambled up massive boulders that looked as though they'd been cut with a knife into perfect blocks. When she'd climbed just below the one Seth was crouched on, she cried, "Where's Emily?"

"Here," said a muffled voice.

One more heave and Beth joined Seth on the rock, to look down with horror at Emily Kuepfer up to her chest in a crevice between two giant boulders.

"Emily!" She choked in horror. "What happened?"

"I slipped." Her upturned face was streaked with tears and sweat. "I can't get out."

"We're getting you out," Seth said grimly. "Come on. Give me your hands."

From far away, Beth heard a throaty whisper, like wind in the grass.

Emily reached up and he grasped her arms below the elbows. Bracing his feet, he pulled.

"Wait!" Emily shrieked. "It hurts—my foot is stuck!"

He relaxed his hold, but Beth was already moving. "I'll see if I can get her loose."

"Beth, do you hear—"

"*Ja,*" she said. "Just focus on Emily right now. And how we're going to get her up to the top of this rockfall if she's really hurt."

On her backside, she slid down to where she estimated Emily's feet must be, and scrabbled for purchase on a rock that tilted like a pair of compasses. There. Emily's sneaker was rammed between two small rocks like a pair of teeth, her ankle twisted awkwardly. Beth grabbed one and tried to rock it to one side, but it was too heavy. With a foot on either side of Emily's leg, she kicked at the other stone. With a crunch, it moved just an inch from a position it had probably occupied since Jesus walked the earth.

"Pull!" she called.

Emily flung up her arms, Seth braced himself, and pulled with all his might.

Emily's sneaker came off and the rocky teeth made sure she paid in blood. But Beth grabbed the sneaker and climbed up the way she'd come.

The whisper of wind in the grass had become people talking in a machine shed after church. A *lot* of people.

"Hurry!" she shouted. "It's coming!" She stuffed the bloody sneaker in her pack and heaved herself onto the rock next to Emily. "Can you walk?"

Emily was crying now. "I don't think so."

"Then we'll carry you. Seth, can you do a fireman's hold?"

"Tell me how." His tone was curt, no-nonsense.

And the people in the machine shed had broken out into a fight, shouting and roaring.

"Emily, I'm going to push you onto his back. Put your arms around his neck, your feet around his hips, and don't break your hold for anything, do you hear me? Seth, when she's secure, I'll help you stand. Then we have to climb like crazy."

He was stronger than she expected. In seconds Emily was secure, her stomach pressed against his spine, her arms locked around his neck in a stranglehold, her bloody feet crossed in front of him, the hurt one hanging down a little.

Boom! Something very large—tree, rock—hit the canyon wall a hundred yards away.

"Go!" Beth screamed, and he scrambled up the side of the nearest boulder on his hands and knees. Beth jammed her skirts into her waistband and scrambled up right behind him. One boulder, two—around the third one and up to the topmost on the rockfall, where she had to put her shoulder under his backside and heave like she'd never heaved before to get the two of them up onto its flat surface.

But the rock—she couldn't get up herself—she was too short—why hadn't she seen that?

With a gasp, she glanced frantically around for a second choice—

"Beth! Hands!"

She flung up her arms, he grabbed her hands, and nearly yanked her arms out of their sockets pulling her up. She scrambled with her feet to help, and they landed in a heap next to Emily just as a wall of water crashed into the curve of the canyon wall and leaped for them.

Beth screamed in terror. Or rather, she felt a raw scream in her throat, but she couldn't hear blessed anything but the thunder of water pouring through the canyon. Water, and downed trees torn up in the maelstrom, and the flotsam of previous flash floods. A poor struggling deer did its best to swim to a bank that was no longer there. It was whirled willy-nilly into an eddy just below them, and by some miracle it found purchase on a now submerged rock. With a single leap, the animal vaulted out of the water, then up on the boulders the same way they had come.

Panting, the doe stood on the rock Beth had just vacated, and didn't seem to be bothered a bit by three horrified pairs of eyes staring down at it.

The water was still rising. Beth threw a glance at Seth. His eyes were wide, but his mouth moved in a soundless prayer.

"Help us, Lord—help us—help us—" she gabbled, but with the noise of shrieking wood and grinding rocks and far too much water in far too small a space, only *der Herr* could hear.

The first boulders in their rockfall had been submerged before the deer came. The second one, just below where Emily had been lodged, went under.

Then it gobbled Emily's toothy rocks, and finally the big one Seth had been standing on, which had to be five feet tall.

Only *Gott* could help them now.

9

AT ANY MOMENT, Seth expected to find himself before the holy throne to meet *der Herr*'s judgment. There was only one thing to do—he knelt on the rock and prayed, doing his best to forgive those who had offended him, as Scripture commanded, and to plead for the souls of the ones he loved. And while he prayed, he heard the roar of the water and at any moment expected to be splashed in the face as it climbed their rock. Even the smaller rocks sounded agonized as they were torn from their comfortable positions and smashed into each other in the depths.

But he and his friends weren't getting wet.

He dared to leave off contemplating the eternal vista and cracked an eye to check on the earthly one.

And blinked.

Beth Stolzfus was calmly pouring clean water from one of the bottles in her day pack on to a nasty, bloody scrape on Emily's right shin, which went all the way from knee to ankle. Emily's face crumpled as she washed out the sand and grit. If his experience was anything to go by, that was going to leave a scar. When the wound was clean, Beth patted it dry with her own skirt and then applied B&W ointment from its little jar. By the time he got his mouth working, with swift hands she'd wrapped Emily's shin with a stretchy bandage and pinned it securely with a safety pin.

It had all taken less than a minute.

This woman clearly did not think that she was going to her judgment today. Like a dam breaking inside him, admiration and what he could only call sheer gratitude washed away a past he was now ashamed of—every time he'd ever made a joke at her expense, or had an uncharitable thought when she made one of her practical remarks or caught him doing something not quite approved by the *Ordnung*.

What a woman. Not one in a hundred would do what she had done in the face of impending death, and then quietly pack her supplies into the little kit and sling the day pack on her shoulders.

"*Denki*, Beth," Emily said over the roar of the water.

"I'm glad I thought to throw this in at the last minute," she replied, and then tilted her head. "Did you hear that?"

All Seth could hear was the agony of the torrent crashing past them. And then he realized he had actually heard her question.

"I can hear you," he said in surprise. "And myself. The water can't be going down already, can it?"

Emily leaned over to take a cautious look. "*Neh*, I'm sorry to say. It's just as high as ever. But not higher. And look. The deer."

Once again three pairs of eyes peered over the edge of the rock. The doe was on edge, moving its feet in agitation, but it was no longer trying to flee for its life. It glanced at them and flicked its ears nervously.

"Don't look directly at her," Seth said. "Look to the side, or she'll spook and probably hurt herself." He took his own advice, and considered the doe out of the corner of his eye. Now that he wasn't in imminent danger of drowning, he picked through the fragments of memory his panicked brain had managed to retain.

"She was swimming toward the rock fall," he said on a note of realization.

"Of course," Beth said. "It was high ground."

"But she let the eddy bring her closer. She didn't fight it or try to get out of it. She *wanted* to come up here because she knows the place."

"And this helps us how?" Emily's voice wobbled. "We're stuck here until the water goes down, however long that takes."

Seth considered the doe, then swiveled his gaze to examine the cliff above.

Realization dawned in Beth's face. "You think she's heading for a game trail. One that will take her out of here."

"It's a possibility, *nix*?"

"Too bad we can't ask her for directions," Emily quipped, clearly doing her best to recover. "Or tie a note around her neck. All our friends probably think we're dead."

Which he had to admit was a fair assessment.

Hooves scraped on the rock. "She's on the move," he said. "Emily, how does your foot feel?"

Tears welled in her eyes. "I'm sorry. I don't think I can put any weight on it. Not enough to climb a game trail."

He grinned. "Then you'll have to borrow my feet, cousin."

He bent, and Beth helped her scramble on to his back, locking her arms and legs as she'd done before. The deer scrambled up the vee made by the rock they stood on and the canyon wall, pushing with her strong hind legs and digging in her hooves. And as she gained a ledge, he realized it was more than just a protrusion.

It was the game trail, right there above them.

"Hang on, Emily. Let's go, Beth. Not fast enough to spook her, but we can't lose her." He set off. "Deer come down to the water to drink every couple of days. But their grazing is up top, on the mesa. If we can stay with her, then we can make our way back along the cliff to that signpost."

"Danger. Steep. Floods," Beth recited, scrambling up on the ledge in front of him. "Understatement of the year."

He felt Emily's chest vibrate in a giggle, and while her weight didn't lessen, his attitude definitely felt lighter.

The trail was barely visible. If it hadn't been for their four-legged guide, even he, who had tracked plenty of game in two states, would have lost it. There simply wasn't enough dirt to hold the impression of passing hooves, but the doe seemed to know her way among the rocks. She even stopped for a minute to crop a clump of dry, end-of-summer grass springing out of a crevice. Up and up she went, diagonally across a canyon wall that wasn't nearly as steep here as it had been on the trail to the petroglyphs.

Denki, mei Vater, for the intelligence and self-preservation of deer. I will be a little more merciful to the ones who try to eat my mother's garden after this.

"I can see the top," Beth gasped, out of breath but clearly determined to do her part and not lag behind the doe.

He had never been so glad to see the sky—it widened and grew the closer they came to the top. But when he looked down to orient himself once again on the trail, he could no longer see the deer.

"She's gone," Emily said sadly next to his ear. "We never got a chance to thank her. I think Beth still has an apple in her day pack we could have given her."

"That doe probably sees two humans in the entire course of a year," Seth said. "She's as wild as a deer gets, and wouldn't eat it, even if you could roll it to her without it falling all the way down the cliff and into the river."

"Good point," Emily said.

Fifteen minutes later, after taking a wrong turn in their eagerness to reach the top, and having to backtrack when it turned out to lead to a crevasse, they emerged at the top of the cliff. The wind grabbed his clothes and nothing had ever felt so good. Seth followed the meandering game trail through the sparse grass with his gaze until he lost it in a cluster of piñon pines. He let Emily slide down his back to the ground, where she managed to stand, most of her weight on her uninjured foot.

"Let's have some water and that apple," he suggested. "I figure we have about a mile before we meet that signpost and turn left toward where Lori parked the van."

"So two hours of walking yet." Emily took the apple from Beth and bit into it. "I'm so sorry, Seth. I wish I'd been more careful." She handed it back to Beth, who took a big bite.

"Don't, cousin. We were all panicked, and it's only *Gottes Hand* that saved us from much worse. Besides, every time your brother Cale does something you don't like, you can tell him his cousin carried you out of a canyon and across the desert because you're the best *Schweschder* in the world."

Emily's laugh was a delight, but Beth's eyes as she handed him the apple for his turn were like a balm to his ragged spirits. The very emotions he had experienced earlier—admiration and gratitude—now glowed in her face.

"We would never have made it if it weren't for you," she said. "You saved our lives, Seth. Again, in my case."

"I think the doe had more to do with that," he said, hoping he wasn't blushing. "If not for her, we'd still be sitting on that rock, wondering how cold it was going to get tonight."

Now Beth laughed, too. "Toss the apple core over into those pines. Maybe she'll find it."

He had just settled Emily on his back and was gathering his strength for the next two hours of walking, when a sound intruded that did not belong in this wide, powerful landscape.

"Is that an engine?" Beth said, shading her eyes to look into the distance. "Didn't Lori say there were no roads in here, to keep the casual tourists out?"

A red four-wheel-drive pickup crested a knoll and bumped toward them. When it pulled up, Seth released a long breath and bent his knees so Emily could stand on her own feet once more.

"You kids lost?" The driver and his two passengers weren't much older than he was. The emblem on the door where his elbow rested said TRIBAL SEARCH & RESCUE.

"If you mean do we know where we're going, then no, we're not lost," Seth said. "If you mean are we glad to see you, we definitely are."

The young man grinned, showing white teeth in a deeply tanned face. "We got a call for a search and *recovery*, so we came loaded with rope and climbing gear and body bags." He hooked a thumb toward the cargo boxes in the back of the pickup. "I'm pretty darned glad it turned out to be a search and *rescue*."

"So are we," Seth said. "I'm Seth, this is my cousin Emily, and our friend Beth."

"Oh, I know your names. Three law enforcement agencies

and the Navajo Tribal Police know them, too. I'm Carson Yazzie, and these comedians are Jimmy and Ernest Begay." His sharp gaze moved to Emily. "You hurt, Emily?"

As he spoke, his two passengers opened the door and jumped down.

"I scraped my leg pretty bad, but my friend here wrapped it," she said. "I think my ankle is sprained. Seth carried me out of the canyon."

Carson's face went slack. "You walked out of Náshdóítsoh Canyon during a flash flood?"

"We got to some high ground, then followed a deer up the game trail just there," Beth said, pointing. "Seth is a good tracker."

One of the Begay brothers whistled. "I'd say so."

The other knelt. "Okay if I examine your ankle?"

She glanced at Beth, as if for permission. At Beth's encouraging nod, she said, "Yes, please."

Seth understood. It wasn't every day an *Englisch* man touched an Amish woman unless he was in the medical profession.

"My friend Jimmy here is an EMT," Carson said. "He'll tell me how fast I have to drive on the way back."

Jimmy's hands were gentle as he examined Emily's ankle. She hung on to Beth for balance. "Nice wrap job," he murmured, almost to himself. Then, "You're right—not broken. Can you put a little weight on it for me, Emily?"

She obeyed, and got her weight nearly balanced on both feet before she gasped and clutched at Beth.

Jimmy glanced up at Carson. "Mild, but painful, and will take a week or two to heal. Still should take her to the clinic. Try and avoid the bumps, okay?"

The driver rolled his eyes. "All right, then. You two girls

ride up front with me. Seth, if you don't mind riding rough in the back, we'll get your cousin to the clinic in town. Sure there's no other injuries?"

"We're sure. Thanks for coming to look for us."

Carson chuckled. "The whole county would have been looking for you if anyone believed you were still alive. We just drew the short straw for the recovery. Okay, hop in, everyone. Ernest, find a repeater and let the others know."

Once he saw Emily and Beth safely into the cab, Seth vaulted over the tailgate and into the back with Jimmy and Ernest. Ernest's handheld radio scratched into life and he reported in that the missing had been found alive and well.

As they bumped back over the mesa in the direction they'd come, Jimmy said, "Was it you wrapped her leg?"

Seth hung on to the side for dear life. "Not me. That was Beth. She's studying to be an EMT."

"That little Amish girl?" Jimmy's eyebrows had risen up under his shaggy black hair.

"That little Amish girl with nerves of steel and a first-aid kit in her day pack," he said with a laugh. "We're from the same town. I've known her for almost a year, and until this trip, it turns out I never knew her at all."

Jimmy's body swayed with the motion of the truck, but he looked almost comfortable on a black bag filled with something soft. Maybe the body bags. Seth pushed the thought away.

His dark eyes examined Seth intently. "So ...?"

What did he mean? "So ... what?"

"A woman like that doesn't come along every day. A cool head in a crisis? Hen's teeth, man. I'd give anything to find a woman like that. So ... what are you going to do about it?"

He was exhausted, filthy, and had just narrowly escaped

death. But anticipation prickled in his blood, and his heart bumped against his ribs as though he were about to run a race. He grinned at Jimmy and Ernest. "Thanks for the slap upside the head. You're absolutely right."

"When are you going to ask her out?" Ernest wanted to know.

"I don't know yet. But I am for sure and certain going to find a way."

GREAT WAS THE REJOICING WHEN LORI PULLED UP OUTSIDE the clinic in the van and all their friends poured out. The poor woman was in tears, apologizing over and over again for leaving them to drown.

It took Seth and Beth ten minutes to calm her down and reassure her that while the danger had been real, they had kept their heads and the *gut Gott* had laid His mighty hand over them in protection.

"And in the end," Seth concluded while Lori blew her nose and tried to recover, "we came away with only a scrape, a mild sprain, and a tale we can tell at family dinners for the rest of our lives."

Emily leaned on her crutches, her ankle wrapped and a fresh bandage on her shin. "The doctor says that if I take it easy for the rest of the trip, I should heal up pretty well. No more hiking for me, I guess."

"If you need to enjoy some wonderful sight, Seth can always carry you up a mountain to get a look," Beth assured her, laughing.

"I can't believe that boy carried her out of the canyon," Lori groaned, unconsciously echoing the Tribal Search &

Rescue crew. "I'm going to have to get out of the tour business. The Yelp reviews from this trip are going to be appalling."

Beth exchanged a grin with Emily. "If any of us were online."

Emily was given the place of honor in the passenger seat next to Lori, so she could prop her foot on the dashboard and keep it elevated. She wasn't in a cast, but she would need to keep the ankle wrapped and iced in order to reduce the swelling. The clinic sent her away with a couple of ice packs she could switch out.

Lori announced that instead of camping, she'd booked rooms in the Navajo-owned motel nearby belonging to the family of her friend. "I know I'm not the only one who could use a proper shower and a real mattress after all this excitement, and Emily needs a solid night's sleep with her leg on a pillow. Since I put you all in danger, I feel I should pick up the tab for your rooms."

They protested, because who except someone who knew the country intimately could have predicted that out of so many hundreds of canyons and arroyos, rainfall so many miles away could have caused a flash flood just at the moment they walked into that particular one? But she was adamant, and in the end Chris and Jeannie gave in.

The family who ran the hotel also ran the restaurant attached to it. Word had already reached them about the Amish people who had escaped the flash flood—which made Seth think that the Amish grapevine had some competition down here in the desert. They pushed four tables together so that everyone could eat and share their stories. It helped that there were only a few other customers, so they welcomed the family to join in the conversation as the food came out.

Chips and salsa Seth was prepared for. But he'd never had

Navajo fry bread, or chile colorado seasoned quite this way, or an avocado, onion, and tomato salad that practically made his eyes roll up in his head.

"This is so *gut*," he moaned. "And it's not hunger sauce, either." He caught the gaze of the mother of the two waitresses, who stood in her chef's apron watching them consume her hard work with the enjoyment that comes of not having to cook it themselves. *"Ahéhee,"* he said to her, pronouncing it the local way Jimmy Begay had told him they said thank you: a-*hyeh*-heh.

The chef's face glowed into a huge smile. "You're most welcome," she said, and circled the table to lay a hand on his shoulder. "My nephews say you are the one who carried your friend out of the canyon."

Seth's face caught fire the way it seemed to every time that got repeated. "I had help." His gaze found Beth's, and for some reason she blushed, too.

Jimmy and Ernest's *Aendi* looked from one to the other, and one winged eyebrow rose. The same way Mamm's did when she knew something and he was too slow on the uptake to get it. Then she nodded. "You did well, both of you. I understand that in your culture pride is wrong, so I will only say that there is more than just one young lady who is grateful. Everyone on the search and rescue team is celebrating tonight along with you. I am glad you chose our family to share yours with."

Catherine and Jeannie began the applause—not for Seth's benefit, for which he was abjectly grateful, but for that of their hosts.

After dessert, which was pistachio ice cream with chocolate syrup over it, the party broke up and the exhausted travelers made their way across a small field fragrant with sage and rabbit bush to the motel. They'd been so long over dinner that twilight had thickened into darkness, but the waning half moon would rise over a distant range of hills pretty soon.

"What was that?" Beth said suddenly, pointing past the fence to open country.

Seth had seen the silvery movement, too. "I think it was a roadrunner."

"He'd better get to bed," she said. "There will be coyotes here."

10

The Mediterranean blue glow of the swimming pool was a siren song irresistible to *some* members of their party.

Jude reached for the snaps on his shirt. "Who's coming in for a swim?"

All the young men except Seth ran into their rooms to strip out of their clothes. Beth was sure not one of them owned or had thought to bring a pair of swim trunks to the desert, but what did that matter when they seemed to have the motel's pool to themselves?

"Last one in is a rotten egg!" Tim hollered, and did a massive cannonball into the deep end. Carl Yutzy and Jude cannoned in right behind him, splashing Jeannie and Delia, who shrieked and ducked away, seconds too late.

Jude whipped his hair out of his eyes and a plume of water arched over his shoulder. "Are you coming in, Miller?"

"Not me," Seth said with a laugh. "I've had just about enough water for today."

"Your loss!" Tim and Carl ducked and swam half the length

of the pool, seeing who could go farthest before surfacing for breath.

The last thing Beth wanted was a bunch of boys in far less clothing than any single woman should singe her eyeballs on, so the sight of Jeannie signaling frantically from the end of their block of rooms was a relief.

Jeannie dragged her into a room with a cement floor and—

"Washing machines!" Beth sighed on a note of ecstasy.

"Run and get your laundry," Janelle said. "I've got Emily's. Tell Catherine, too."

"What about the boys?"

"Seth will help Carl round all theirs up. Though in my opinion, if they'd rather launder themselves than their clothes, they deserve to wear dirty pants for the rest of the trip."

Alden had always helped their mother and then Beth herself with the family's laundry, though there were men in the *Gmay* who disapproved of a boy doing women's work. What some folks didn't realize was that sometimes, cowboying or simply the absence of the women of the household for a visit or a trip required knowing how to work a washer, whether that was *Englisch* or Amish. On some ranches, especially *Englisch* ones, Alden had told her, no woman at the big house would do the hands' laundry. That was up to them, even if it meant hitching a ride into town with their duffel bag. Her brother had a healthy respect for what his mother and sisters did for him.

Most of the boys, according to Carl, hadn't brought more than two pairs of pants and three shirts. She could imagine Seth's pants had suffered more than a little from that climb up the canyon with Emily on his back.

As if her thoughts had signaled him, he hustled into the laundry room with his soiled pants and shirts just as Beth and

Janelle were feeding coins into the washer. Janelle spotted him in the doorway. "This is such a treat," she said. "Imagine having an entire load of clothes done in ninety minutes. I am going to be so spoiled."

"Can I throw mine in?" He held up his bundle.

"Of course," Beth said, and pointed to a second washer. "That's the one we're using for the darks—pants and kitchen aprons and socks. It's still filling."

He stuffed in the clothes and Beth followed it with soap. "Where's Emily? I haven't seen her since supper."

"She's gone to bed," Janelle said. "Her ankle has had all it can take. In fact, now that these are going, I'm going to check on her." She slipped out.

With two washers going full tilt, there wasn't much for Beth to do for the next forty-five minutes. But Seth didn't follow Emily out. Instead, he hovered, looking uncertain and nervous. She couldn't remember ever seeing him that way before.

"Beth, could I talk to you for a minute?"

She looked over at him curiously, keeping her hands busy folding the plastic shopping bags the girls had brought the laundry in, then lifted one shoulder in a shrug. "Sure." She followed him out into the parking lot. "I hope you're not going to try to convince me to go swimming."

He made a derisive noise in his throat. "I can't even convince *me* to go swimming. The guys tried to, but I'm done with water for today. Even if it's well behaved and trapped in a pool."

"So far this trip, I haven't seen any well-behaved water," she said wryly. "I have a whole new appreciation for the creek back home. Even Siksika Lake is looking good to me now."

As they reached the gap between the motel and the restaurant, a slight glow illuminated the horizon, which was probably the moon thinking about rising. "The Begays' *Aendi* at the restaurant mentioned something about a circle," he said. "If neither of us want to swim, what about taking a walk?"

The shock reverberated through her as though she were a gong struck by a mallet. "Don't you think we've had enough walking, too?" she blurted. No, that sounded like a refusal. "Mind you," she added hastily, "it's a lot less than we would've had if Carson Yazzie and the Begays hadn't come along at just the right moment."

"Not for the exercise. Just to simmer down enough to sleep."

That sounded reasonable. It wasn't a date or anything. Just a walk, for practical reasons. She turned with him, and they walked slowly across the open field toward what looked like a cluster of rocks or a knoll. Creosote bush brushed at her skirts and sage released a scent that reminded her of the way their kitchen smelled at Thanksgiving and *Grischtdaag*.

"Sunday tomorrow," he said. "Do you suppose Jeanne and Chris will have church?"

"I was wondering about that." Beth rubbed a leaf of sage and inhaled the stronger scent. "Catherine told me that when they were at Glacier, they just had a short singing and Chris offered a prayer. Maybe it will be the same tomorrow."

"I guess we could sing in the van as we drive. I don't know how much that would invite the *Heilige Geist*, though. Don't think the Spirit would be very comfortable zooming down the highway in a van."

"The Spirit is supposed to be in us, not the van," she said with a smile. "If I had my way, I'd walk out here in the early morning, and sing the *Loblied*, right about the time they would be singing it at home." She kept her voice light. But while she actually meant it, she also knew the idea was was not quite suitable and maybe even a little scandalous.

"I'm sure Jeanne and Chris have put some thought into that." With a sigh, he gazed out to the horizon, where the glow was getting stronger. Above them, in the inky vault of the sky, a river of stars swam from one side of infinity to the other. "Look. The Milky Way."

She looked up, and her lips parted at the beauty of it. "We can see the Milky Way and even the Northern Lights at home, but not as clearly as this."

"Not so much moisture in the air here."

"I can't believe it was only this morning that we were looking at the sunrise through Mesa Arch. It seems like a year ago."

"For sure and certain," he agreed. "Look—over there. There really is a circle. Or half a one, anyhow. The family must come out here to enjoy it."

There was just enough light from the Milky Way to see an arc of four or five hand-split benches, held up by rocks that had clearly come from the tumble a short distance away.

"I think we just found our place to have church, if the Begays say it's all right," she said. "The view must be beautiful in the daytime."

Seth lowered himself to the bench on the end with a groan. "That hike up the canyon wall is catching up to me."

"I have some muscle ointment in my kit," she said, feeling a little shy as she settled on the same bench, a respectable foot or so between them. "I'll give it to you when we get back."

Massaging both calves, he tilted his head to look at her. "Is there anything you don't have in that kit?"

"Splints?"

"If it turns out we need those, we're in more trouble than we thought."

She nodded. "I'd say so. Have I thanked you for this afternoon? I've never been more terrified in my life. That river—"

For a moment, he was silent. "What is it with you and rivers? You didn't look terrified. I was on my knees preparing to meet *der Herr*, and there you were, doing first aid."

"What is it with you saving my life?" she quipped. "We wouldn't have got out of there without you."

"The doe saved us, not me. I mean it, Beth. How do you stay so cool in a crisis?"

He really wanted to know. She could hear it in his voice. He wasn't just teasing her, or storing up whatever she said to bring up in front of people later. Maybe it was time for honesty, out here in a place that felt sacred. Protected.

"I had to focus on Emily's leg or go into a complete panic. Every muscle in my body wanted to run away screaming, or throw myself into that maelstrom just to get the inevitable over with."

"But that would have been a sin."

"I know. The urge went as soon as it came. I couldn't do a blessed thing to save myself—but there was something I could do for someone else. I had B&W, I had a bandage, I had someone who needed me. That settled me down and let me get on with helping her." She took a shaky breath. It was going to be a while before the memories of those moments faded enough to live with.

"Seems like you have the perfect qualifications to be an EMT."

Her laugh was more like a puff of air. "I hope so. I really want to get my license. And be able to help the *Gmay*, like Sara Fischer does."

"We can never have too many with those skills. I think it's a fine thing you're doing."

Thank goodness he couldn't see her blush in the dark. "I haven't done it yet."

"You will."

A silence fell, filled with the sound of the wind rustling in the rabbit bush, and a *chip-chip* sound that might have been a small animal or bird of some kind, alarmed at the presence of humans.

This was a trip in which anything could happen. And had. And might yet, if she had the courage. She took a breath to speak.

"Beth, can I say something?"

She exhaled. "Of course. There's no one here but me and whatever is making that noise over there."

All she could see under the brim of his hat was half a smile —and the shadow of a tiny dimple no bigger than a seed at the corner of his mouth. "I don't think we want to know what that is." Then his mouth turned serious. "Beth ... if—when we get home, would you let me drive you home from singing some Sunday night?"

For the second time that night, shock rendered her speechless.

His voice hurried into the blowing silence. "It's okay to say *neh*. It's so strange ... this trip ..." He seemed to gather himself. Which was more than she was able to do. "It's like I've just met you. And realized I've never known anyone like you."

"Me, too. Known anyone like you, I mean."

"Then ... maybe we can start again." He held out a hand. "Hallo, I'm Seth Miller. I'm from New Mexico, and I'm cowboying at the Circle M Ranch for *mei Onkel*. I go to church with them in the west district, except when I'm at my *mamm*'s place in the east district."

She took his hand. It was lean and strong. Just the right kind of hand for a man who climbed canyons with injured people on his back. She gave it a shake and released it.

"I'm Beth Stolzfus," she replied. "I was born in Whinburg Township, and I mostly look after the house for my mother, except when she needs me in the quilt shop. I'm studying to be an EMT, and we go to church in the east district, too."

"Maybe I'll be at Mamm's more often in the future, then."

The future. What did he hope *der Herr* planned for his future? "Did you always want to be a cowboy?"

"It was less about wanting than being needed," he said thoughtfully. "We had five hundred acres in New Mexico and grazed cattle. I learned to ride as soon as my feet would reach the stirrups—I wanted to be like my brothers and my father. Dat was a *gut* rider. Watching him cutting calves out of a herd was like ... well, it was as precise as my mother cutting an onion. Not a movement wasted. Kind of beautiful in its own way. Well, I wanted to be as good as he was. I was well on the way when he died."

"That was five years ago, wasn't it?"

"Seems like a lot less than that some days, and an eternity in others. Anyway, the church gradually dwindled away until it was just us and the bishop's family, and then we came out here for Christmas for a visit, along with the Kuepfers. Mamm took one look at the Inn and that was that. We sold the ranch to the millionaire next door, and moved here in February."

"And you plan to stay on the Circle M?"

"If they'll have me. But..."

She waited.

"Once Adam and Zach get their houses finished, Reuben

and Daniel won't have as much need for Gideon and me. Not sure what I'll do then."

"If you could do anything at all, what would it be?"

"Besides go to California and swim in the ocean?"

She tilted away a little to stare at him. "Really?"

He chuckled and shook his head. "I used to dream about that. And about riding the train and never getting off. Just going everywhere and seeing everything. Not being tied down."

"Sounds lonely." She could have said a lot more, but that was the thing that struck her most. That and how un-Amish it sounded. But Seth was baptized. He couldn't be thinking of jumping the fence, could he?

"I see that now." He sighed. "This trip was supposed to satisfy that urge. To find out what lies over the horizon, you know?"

"We've seen a fair number of horizons," she allowed. "But mostly it makes me appreciate the mountains around the Siksika Valley. Eternal. Protective."

"Snowy."

"It's nice to have something you can count on."

He laughed, and examined his loosely clasped hands between his knees. "Maybe that's part of what made me look away instead of nearby. I was born on the ranch, after Mamm and Dat decided to move to New Mexico to help establish a church there. The ranch was all I'd ever known, and ranching was all Dat had ever known. After he died, it felt like everything I'd ever thought was forever was being taken away. My friends in church, leaving. The ranch, when Mamm told us she couldn't keep it running on her own, even with all of us helping. And then when we got here, and Luke came back to the valley, it felt like I couldn't count on her, either."

"But you can," she said softly. "You know that, don't you?"

"*Ja*, we all can. Luke is *gut* for her, and it's *wunderbaar* that she's so happy again." He sucked in a breath and sat up, as though a thought had struck him. "Little Joe will be publishing their wedding in church tomorrow. And I'm going to miss it."

She dared to bump his shoulder with her own. "It's not like it isn't common knowledge, Seth. You're not really missing anything—and you and Gideon will be his *Neuwesitzern, ja?*"

He nodded. "First Tobias, now Mamm. Gid and I are getting to be old hands at this. But Luke doesn't have anyone else. I'm glad to stand in that place for him." After a moment, he said, "What about you? How old were you when you left Whinburg Township? Did you want to go?"

"*Ach, ja,*" she said. Understatement of the year. "We couldn't wait to get away."

Now it was his turn to lean out a little to look at her. Then he crossed his ankles and leaned back on his hands. "Sounds like a story."

"Not a very happy one."

"If you don't want to tell me, *ischt okay*. Look, here's the moon."

The silver edge of the half moon glowed over the horizon and began its slow climb into the sky. Now she could see his face a little more clearly. Calm, unjudgmental. Giving her space to make up her own mind.

"We ... didn't have a very happy childhood, Alden and Julie and me. Not because of Mamm," she added hastily. "We couldn't ask for a better mother. But Dat ... he..." She took a breath. She'd never spoken these words to anyone. Not even Julie, who had lived through it. "He believed in discipline."

"So did my father." It sounded like a question.

"But he really believed in it. If I didn't set the table properly, he hit my hands with the butter knife and make me do it all over again. Nothing I did was ever right. Not one thing. School was an escape and I loved going. But if I brought home something that wasn't ten out of ten, he'd rage and call me stupid. If Mamm tried to reason with him, or remind him I was just a child, and childhood was meant for learning, he'd hit her. If Julie wanted to go to the pond to see if they needed another body on the ice, he'd lock her in her room for being worldly. Alden—" An involuntary shudder crept up her spine. "He had it worse than we did. The only son. The one who was supposed to be perfect. He apprenticed to Dat in the blacksmith shop. There were days when he'd come in for dinner and his eyes would be haunted. I couldn't bring myself to ask what had happened."

Seth let out a long breath, as if he'd been holding it. "So you left?"

"My father cut across a field one morning to borrow something from the neighbor. He didn't know the man had bought a bull at the auction the day before."

Seth made an inarticulate sound.

"After the funeral, we left. There were too many bad memories. I felt sorry for the family who bought our house—I mean, I don't believe in ghosts, but there were times I'd walk into a room and remember every bad thing that had happened there. I believe places can be haunted. By memories. Or by emotions."

Silently, he closed the little space between them on the bench and took her hand. "I'm so sorry."

"It's all in the past," she whispered. "Where it belongs. But sometimes—" She swallowed. "I'm afraid I don't take criticism very well, even though it's been years. Even the mildest words make me feel like he's standing over me again with the butter knife."

"*Ach*, Beth." The sound of her name was like a balm to her aching spirit. "I'm pretty sure I've been guilty of making you feel that way."

"Maybe once or twice." His hand around hers tightened and nothing had ever felt more comforting. "But let that go into the past, too. We've just met, remember?"

"And here I am holding your hand. My mother would be shocked."

"*I'm* shocked. In a *gut* way," she finished softly.

"Does that mean I get to drive you home from singing?"

"You don't have a buggy."

"I can borrow one."

"Then *ja*, I'd be happy to ride home with you. And isn't that forward of me?"

11

SUNDAY, SEPTEMBER 18

WORD FILTERED through the ranks of the *Youngie* from their chaperones that they had permission from the Begays to meet out on the cliff for worship at eight o'clock, the usual time the church service began at home. When she was showered and dressed, and her nearly white *Kapp* on over her hair instead of the *Duchly*, Beth thanked whatever unknown person who'd had the amazing idea of supplying each room with a coffee maker and envelopes of coffee. It took her, Catherine, and Janelle a minute to figure out how to make it work, but since no one had thought yesterday about breakfast today and bought groceries, it was a start. The restaurant would open for breakfast while they were out on the cliff, but until they returned, as long as there was coffee, Beth figured she would survive.

The sun had come up long ago, its rays stretching across the brush and red dirt as they walked out to the half-circle of benches. Jude and Tim ventured close to the edge of the cliff and peered over, only to beat a hasty retreat back to safety.

"A hundred feet straight down into a canyon," Tim

murmured to Seth, as they seated themselves on either side of Beth and Catherine.

Beth decided that was one view she'd enjoy from twenty feet away. Goodness knew it was a spectacular sight, the red mesas lifting from the desert floor to catch the sunlight, the piñon pines making rivers of green in the drainages, and above it all, a sky the intense blue of a September morning.

Chris cleared his throat, and in a moment the first notes of "Great is Thy Faithfulness" rose into the air. Beth understood at once that this hour of worship would be more like a singing than a service, but there was beauty in the old *Englisch* hymns, too. Especially when they reached the second verse.

> *Summer and winter and springtime and harvest,*
> *Sun, moon, and stars in their courses above*
> *Join with all nature in manifold witness*
> *To thy great faithfulness, mercy, and love.*

Der Herr had certainly been faithful in preserving them from the raging torrent of the flash flood. And nature had not only been their witness, it had come to their rescue in the shape of the doe, leading them away from destruction the way Jesus led a person out of a destructive world.

"Morning by morning new mercies I see," she sang. She turned her head just a fraction and there was Seth, singing with one corner of his mouth quirked up, as though he, too, appreciated this morning so much it might have been that very first one that had made *der Herr* see that it was good.

The second hymn on a Sunday morning was always the *Loblied.* Chris, as their impromptu *Vorsinger*, sang the first line. They joined in on the second and sang the hymn every Amish person knew by heart, sung as it was in every church service.

When their voices died away on the wind twenty minutes later, Chris rose to his feet. He clasped his hands again and again, as though he felt the responsibility of leading a service, even though he was no ordained bishop or appointed deacon.

"Let us pray," he said, the words trembling a little in contrast to the confidence of his singing. "Lord our Father in Heaven, we thank Thee for Thy mighty hand in delivering us from the river yesterday. We thank Thee for preserving Emily's life through the help and strength of our friends. We thank Thee for the words of the prophet Isaiah, who said, *'For in the wilderness shall waters break out, and streams in the desert.'* Who said, *'And a highway shall be there, and a way, and it shall be called the way of holiness.'"* Chris took a breath and went on. *"'The unclean shall not pass over it; but it shall be for those: the wayfaring men, though fools, shall not err therein.'"*

In this solemn moment, Beth felt Catherine's shoulders shake in a sudden fit of giggles. The wayfaring men, though fools, indeed! For sure and certain they'd been fools to explore too far down that canyon—and now the prophet was speaking across the centuries to tell them so. Beth pressed both hands over her mouth to stifle her own giggles, and elbowed Catherine in the ribs to make her stop.

But nothing made a person laugh harder than trying not to laugh. Oh goodness, she mustn't!

And then Seth looked over, probably because he felt Catherine's shoulders shaking, too, and caught Beth red-faced, tears of laughter welling in her eyes.

On her other side, Tim elbowed her just in time before she lost control completely. And it sobered her up enough to remember she was twenty-two, not twelve. Surreptitiously, she wiped the tears out of the corners of her eyes and hoped to goodness no one else had heard their muffled noise.

"Keep us safe for the rest of this journey, Lord. Be with our families and friends at home, pour out Thy spirit on them on this Thy day. We thank Thee for Thy keeping, and help us to show Thy love and spirit to others until we are safe home again. In the name of Thy Son we pray. Amen."

"Amen," Beth murmured.

The next hymn was her favorite, and the one she chose at singing when she got the chance—"How Great Thou Art." It seemed to fit the day and this place, whose benches may even have been built so a person might consider what the Creator had made.

They followed it with one of the hymns from the *Ausbund* they usually sang at the end of the service, before people were dismissed to go outside. As they rose, it almost seemed a shame to break the peace by saying anything. In ones and twos, Beth watched these *Youngie* who had become her friends walk slowly out of the half circle, soaking in the sun and a view that certainly reminded a person how small a part they played in the Creator's great work.

"Okay now?" Seth murmured next to her, gazing out into the fields of air beyond the cliff edge.

"Mamm would be ashamed of me," she whispered. "But it was so funny—the wayfaring men! Fools! That was totally us."

"Chris was certainly studying that Bible in the nightstand," Seth agreed. "I bet it took him half the night to find the perfect verses."

Now a giggle bubbled freely out of her. "And they were perfect. Though I think I have a bruise where Tim gave me the elbow. He's going to make a *gut* father, keeping order among the *Kinner* in church."

Seth barked a laugh. "I won't tell him you said that. *Kumm mit.* It looks like everyone is heading over to the restaurant for breakfast."

Lori had given them privacy for their service, choosing instead to sleep in. They found her at the big table they had used the night before. She waited until everyone had their order and taken the initial edge off their hunger before tapping her fork on her water glass. "I wanted to talk about the next day or two of our trip."

"We're not leaving today, are we?" Jeannie Kauffman asked, sounding plaintive. "Sundays are a day of rest, and I think Emily should definitely rest. She needs to keep her foot up and put ice on it at regular intervals. We can't do that if we're on the road."

"I agree," Lori said placidly, spooning salsa on her fried potatoes. "I was thinking of tomorrow."

Even Emily, who disliked people making a fuss, looked relieved.

"The plan was to drive down to Page and visit Antelope Canyon, the famous slot canyon. We'd need to make arrangements with the tribe for a tour—we have to have a Navajo guide," she added. "You can't just walk in there like you can at some of the other national monuments and state parks."

"What's a slot canyon?" Carl Yutzy wanted to know.

"Think of Náshdóítsoh Canyon—" Lori began.

"I've been trying not to," Delia said.

"Don't do that," Beth encouraged her softly. "Before the flash flood, it was lovely. It deserves to be remembered."

"Think of Náshdóítsoh Canyon," Lori repeated, "and shrink it until it's only a little wider than your shoulders, and shallow enough that three of you could stand on one another's shoulders and maybe touch the top if you were lucky. Now take that narrow canyon and twist and flute it so it looks like fabric gathered up and furled."

Eleven sets of eyes stared at her.

In the silence, Auntie Begay took a calendar off the wall and brought it over to the table. "This is one time when a picture will be worth a thousand words, and even then will not do it justice. We call it Tsé Bíghanílíní, the place where water runs through rocks. It's a holy place."

Beth leaned over to look as the calendar, each month bearing a fresh picture of the canyon, went slowly around the table. When Auntie Begay took it away into the kitchen again, Emily was already shaking her head.

"I can't," she croaked. "Leaving my ankle out of it, I'm a big chicken. Even as *wunderbaar* as it looks, I can't go down in there. Not after yesterday."

"There's no water," Lori assured her. "It was carved by wind and water and sand, but that was thousands of years ago."

"I can't, either," Delia said. "But there's no reason the rest of you can't go."

"It does look amazing," Beth said slowly. The photographs had been mind-boggling in their beauty. Someday maybe she'd be able to return and see it with her own eyes.

"It's a wonder of the world," Lori told them, "and I do not exaggerate. But everyone in the van ought to agree. If you don't, well, the canyon has been there a long time. It will be waiting for you if you come back again."

"So ... on to the Grand Canyon tomorrow, then?" Chris asked.

"Yes," Lori said. "But for today, swim and walk if you want to. Write a postcard. Or do absolutely nothing."

"I can't remember the last time I did absolutely nothing," Beth murmured to Janelle, next to her. "Maybe never."

"I saw boxes of jigsaw puzzles by the reception desk," she said. "Maybe Emily and I will do one. Want to join us?"

"*Denkes*, but I think I'll take a couple of postcards out to where we had church and write home."

Dear Mamm,

This has been the most amazing trip. So far I've fallen in a river in one state and narrowly avoided a flash flood in another. If it wasn't for Seth Miller I don't know where I'd be. Today we had church on a cliff and it was wonderful. On to the Grand Canyon tomorrow.

Much love—Beth

She read it over, wondering if Mamm would be glad to hear from her, or panicked about the unruly rivers she kept encountering. And maybe mentioning Seth hadn't been very wise, either. Since she'd been keeping company with Willard, Mamm tended to see romance in everything from bees to trees.

Which was *wunderbaar* in its own way. If anyone deserved a little happiness after the fire of tribulation, it was her mother. And the expression in Willard's eyes as he looked at her, or brought lunch he'd made from scratch to the quilt shop, or did yet another of the endless repairs around their house just so he could see her smile ... well, Beth and Julie predicted there would be another wedding sooner rather than later.

She put a pebble on the postcard so it wouldn't blow away, and picked up the next.

Dear Willard,

Some day I hope you can take a trip like this and eat some of the amazing food in the southwest. Last night we had Navajo fry bread and chile colorado in a restaurant and it was the best. Mostly we cook

*in camp, but that was a real treat. I'll try to get the recipes, and share
them with you.*

Love—Beth

Love Beth. A year ago, the very thought of writing such a
thing to old bachelor Willard Zook would have been impossible. Willard and his brother Hezekiah were inseparable in
people's minds, to the point that the girls joked that if you
took one, you had to take the pair, like socks. But Beth knew
differently now. Will's love for her mother and for her *Kinner*
was like a stoked woodstove, comforting and dependable and a
protection from the storms outside.

She addressed both cards and wondered if Auntie Begay
also sold stamps.

"Am I interrupting?"

She looked up to see Seth standing hesitantly at the end of
the bench she was sitting on. "*Neh*, I've just finished. I'm going
to send these to Mamm and Willard." She waved them, the
bright orange and red and green of the photograph on the
front a pretty good depiction of the colors in the mesas at
sunset.

"I wondered if you felt like a walk. Jude, Tim, and Carl
can't stay out of the pool. They warned me that if I set foot on
the deck, they'd toss me in, clothed or not."

"For being in the desert, we sure spend a lot of time
avoiding water," she said wryly. "Sure, a walk would be nice."
She kept her tone casual. Both of them were well aware that a
walk held significance just a few degrees short of a ride home
from singing. If you wanted to be alone with someone yet in
full, decorous view, you might ask them to go for a walk. It
could be the act of a friend, or a precursor to a courtship.

But at the moment, there was no one else out here. It

might be early afternoon and broad daylight, but they were as alone as if they were in a buggy at midnight.

"What are you thinking?" Seth asked, walking on her left, between her and the cliff edge.

For a second, she thought about saying she needed some stamps. But that was something the old Beth would say—something practical and off-putting that would discourage him enough that he'd go away. That was before being brutally baptized in the Madison River. Before the sunrise at Mesa Arch. And, of course, before Náshdóítsoh Canyon.

"I was just thinking we're as alone out here as we would be in a buggy on the way home from singing. Only with a whole lot less teasing beforehand."

"It may come afterward. Jude has been relentless with the hints and remarks, and now Tim is catching on."

"There are worse things in life than being teased about you."

"Denki," he said flippantly, but he looked pleased. "So you're writing a postcard to Willard. Does that mean he's becoming part of the family?"

"You've seen my mother when they're together. What do you think?"

"I think he deserves a whole letter."

She laughed as she slipped the postcards into the pocket of her apron. "But as we learned at breakfast, a picture is worth a thousand words, and the one on the postcards is pretty good. I'm hoping Auntie Begay will let me have a recipe or two to take home and share with him."

"He'd love that. No turquoise knife handle or fancy boots for Willard. Give him a recipe he hasn't seen before, and he'll be your friend forever."

They meandered along the cliff, alternating between the

view over the mesas and the nearly as interesting sight of the tumble of rocks they were approaching. Close up, it was the size of a small hill.

"I wonder what happened here?" Some of the rocks were bigger than both of them put together. "It looks similar to that rockfall we were marooned on before the deer came."

"Maybe it was a sandstone formation that finally gave up and fell over." Seth leaned in to inspect a cleanly split face. "Beth, look at this."

She joined him, peering at the rock face. "Is that ... a pictograph?" In the red of the rock was a darker, browner color. A splotch. No— "A spiral," she breathed. "Out here where anyone can see it. Are there more?"

On another smooth face, he found a second. And next to it, a chevron-like drawing that might have been a cornstalk.

"I feel like we've discovered buried treasure," he said, delight suffusing his face. "What was it Auntie Begay told us— that the spiral acted like a kind of calendar for the longest and shortest days of the year."

"Maybe in the past, they farmed corn here." Beth shaded her eyes with her hand and considered the clifftop. "I'm so glad you didn't go swimming. We'd never have seen these, especially when the sun moves enough to throw a shadow on these rock faces."

"I can always go swimming at home. Out here, even a walk is an adventure."

"That's what I wanted on this trip," she said. "Funny how I always seem to find it with you. Nothing ever happens when I'm with Carl or Jude. Or Tim."

"Didn't Carl want you to sit with him, or is my memory giving out on me?"

She wrinkled her nose at him. "Maybe. But there are

people I'd rather sit with. He's not much older than me, but I think his brain is the same age as Tim's little brother."

As he smiled, there was that tiny dimple next to the corner of his mouth. She decided she'd better watch where she was going instead, so he wouldn't catch her staring.

"I guess you can be grateful for friends like them," he said easily. "You need the calm between the storms, *nix?*"

"Calm has its place, like this morning. But adventure definitely gives me stories to tell my family—once they can see with their own eyes that I survived." Again, she had second thoughts about sending the postcard to Mamm. But she had to have survived if she could write it, *nix?*

"I'll be glad to see our own mountains again," he admitted, surprising her.

"Not hankering for California beaches?"

He huffed a laugh that sounded like disbelief. "Not really. I mean, how can they compete with Náshdóítsoh Canyon?"

Somewhere deep inside, Beth felt a little glow of happiness. Leaving out the scary parts, maybe these moments they'd shared together could be the beginning of something. If he was letting go of old dreams, maybe new ones could come in and take their place.

New ones that might include her.

❧ 12 ❧

MONDAY, SEPTEMBER 19

WHEN THEY CLIMBED into the van after breakfast the next morning, Seth was sorry to leave the Begay family, who had been kindness itself. When he mentioned that he and Beth had found two of the pictographs in the rockfall, Uncle Begay had smiled as if they shared a secret.

"Don't tell the tourists," he murmured. "That place is special to our family. We only like to share it with our friends."

Seth felt as though he'd been given a gift. Because the quiet clifftop with the benches and the rockfall had felt special to him, too. And the fact that whatever sacred echoes still presided over the place had permitted him and Beth to see the pictographs was even more of a gift.

He tossed his bag, now filled with clean clothes, with a postcard tucked in among them, up to Chris and then climbed into the van. Beth had claimed the window seat in the very back, and before Carl Yutzy even reached the door, Seth had settled into the seat next to her.

"If you were looking for a calm, quiet ride, I can trade with him," he murmured as Carl and Janelle filled the remaining two seats in the row.

"Not me," she murmured back. "But I'll pray for an uneventful four hundred and some miles, all the same. I think we owe it to our friends not to invite another adventure."

He couldn't help his grin. How had he never noticed her dry sense of humor before this trip? Maybe because he'd never really heard her talk much before. And maybe, given what she'd shared with him the night of the moonrise, she'd never dared to let it out before. From what he understood of the unhappy man who had been her father, humor would have been seen as talking back, or even disrespect, and punished.

How lucky he and his siblings were to have had Marlon Miller for a father!

How long had he been feeling sorry for himself because *Gott* had called his *dat* home before he, Seth, was ready? How long had he silently blamed Mamm for selling the ranch that was the only home he'd ever known ... when the reality was that trying to keep it running had been a losing battle? Tobias had told him and Gideon so, frankly and without drama, before they moved. And Seth had chosen to believe his own fear, his own sense of all these losses piling up, instead of the reality that their family needed something to live on both physically and spiritually. A move to the Siksika, where Dat's brother could help them, and Mamm already knew many in the church, had been the only sensible choice. And Mamm, being a sensible woman, had invited them all to make the choice with her.

Oh, he'd gone along with it. But he'd resented it. And worse, he'd learned not to count on things to stay the same. Or to depend on people, even those closest to him. He was beginning to see now how dangerous that was. How easy it would be to drift out of fellowship. If nothing else, the flash flood had taught him how vital fellowship and interdependence was. If each of them had depended only on themselves, someone would have died.

As they pulled out, waving to the Begay family standing outside the restaurant, he knew for sure and certain that *Gott* had spoken to him. He needed to make some changes. To begin with, when he got home, he would make it up to his mother somehow. Especially with her and Luke's wedding coming up in two weeks.

Beside him, Beth's eyes fluttered open at the conclusion of her prayer. Her lashes were thick and stubby, and under her *Duchly*, her brown hair shone with a fresh washing.

She found him studying her, and her cheeks flushed. "Please tell me I don't have dirt on my face."

"Of course not. That bee on your *Duchly*, now—"

She sucked in a breath and swiped frantically at her head covering. "Where? Get it off! Where is it?"

He put a hand on her wrist. "I was joking. No bees. Not even a fruit fly. I'm sorry."

She relaxed, but with the other hand, she patted down the rest of her headscarf and her neck just in case. And somehow, his remained on her wrist.

Then slid down until his fingers found hers, palm to palm.

Half of him was certain she'd treat his hand like the bee —*get it off!* But she didn't. Instead, her color deepened and their clasped hands lowered to the seat between them, where the others couldn't see.

For a hundred miles, they didn't say a word. They didn't need to. Because Seth had never realized before how much ordinary skin and fingers and palms could say all on their own.

He'd held hands with girls before, of course. Okay, two girls. Once in New Mexico and twice with Sharon Keim.

But in neither case had it been like this. Electric. His entire consciousness was focused on the slightest movement of her fingers. The difference in the texture of her skin between her palm and the back of her hand. The way their hands seemed to fit together, though his fingers were longer and hers were softer. He had calluses from fencing and tack and throwing hay. She had short nails, probably because longer ones would interfere with work. Sharon's were longer, and filed into ovals. Once, when he'd taken her for ice cream in Mountain Home, she'd told him she'd put clear nail polish on and had gone two whole days before anyone noticed.

He doubted it would ever occur to Beth to put on nail polish.

He wondered why he had ever thought Sharon Keim would be the woman to make him happy. What would she have done up on that rockfall while a flash flood raged mere feet below her? Hard to imagine, but it wouldn't be good.

"Penny for your thoughts?" Beth whispered.

"I was just thinking about Sharon Keim."

Her entire body went stiff, and her hand slid out of his.

But he was too quick—too unwilling to let her go. He caught it back—and if he had challenged her to arm wrestle him, the result would have been the same against the wall of her resistance.

"Your fingernails, you see," he said, pretending to look past her at the scenery while it was all he could do to hang on. "You keep them short for work, *nix?*"

"*Ja.*" It sounded pretty close to the warning cats gave you before lashing out with claws bared. "Let go of me."

"Did you know she paints her nails?"

"I hope you like them."

"That's the thing. What kind of Amish woman paints her nails and walks around for days daring someone to notice? Kathryn Keim finally did, and told her she'd better get it off before Sunday. That's when Sharon found out you have to buy a whole different bottle of nail polish *remover* to do that." He shook his head. "Now she's got two bottles of stuff she can't use. How does that make sense?"

"Are you trying to make me feel bad?" she whispered, giving up the struggle. Her hand now lay in his like a trout on the bank after the gaff.

"I would never do that." He wanted to kiss that poor hand, but he restrained himself. "I'm just discovering that I am the biggest *Narr* ever to walk the earth. I had such a crush on that girl, and now I'm wondering what I ever saw in her. Jimmy Begay was right. *A woman like that doesn't come along every day*, he told me. He was talking about you."

"Me," she said in a tone that said, *One of you is certainly narrisch.*

"Yep. He was practically ready to propose."

She rolled her eyes in a way that implored heaven for patience.

"I guess what I'm getting at is that no woman I've ever met holds a candle to you, Beth Stolzfus."

"Not even Sharon Keim." Her voice was flat.

"Especially not Sharon Keim. And her painted nails. And her giggle. And her desperation."

"Don't be mean."

"I'm not. Every word of that is the truth and you know it."

She tilted her chin in a way that acknowledged he might be right, and her fingers showed some signs of life in his. "If I were a matchmaker, I would put her and Dave Yoder together."

"Oh, now who is being mean?" he teased.

"*Neh*, truly. He would spend the rest of his life being grateful, and she would probably learn some sense. Dave has enough sense for two. It's just the way he shares it that's obnoxious."

That was one way of putting it. He squeezed her hand. "Forgive me?"

She met his penitent gaze and squeezed back. "Of course. Forgive me for flying off the handle."

"I'm glad you've never challenged me to an arm wrestle. I might lose."

She tilted her chin. "Let that thought keep you humble."

And then she flicked a fold of her burgundy dress over their clasped hands and settled back in the comfortable seat. A highway mileage sign flashed past. "Three hundred miles left to go."

"Not enough," he whispered, running his thumb the length of hers under cover of the fabric. "Not nearly enough."

THEY ARRIVED AT THE CAMPGROUND TOO LATE TO GO INTO the park, what with a shopping trip for groceries and Jude and Janelle attempting a dinner that was a little bit beyond both of them. But Jeannie Kauffman took pity on her brother-in-law and stepped in to help, with the result that instead of their fish chowder being stuffed into pastry shells, they simply had chowder and biscuits.

"If they hadn't made such a fuss about their failure," Beth

said quietly to Seth as they ate on a pair of stumps near the campfire, "we all would have thought it was a success."

"Is there a lesson in that?" he mused around a mouthful. "Because it's definitely a success."

"I'm not sure," she said with a small smile. "Misery might love company, but failure loves comfort. At least, mine always did. I hope the sight of everyone enjoying dinner is a comfort." Goodness knew she'd lived with more failure than she knew what to do with. "I can sympathize, though. Even now, it's hard for me to try new things. My father's voice comes out of nowhere and tries to ruin them. Makes me feel like whatever I choose will be pointless, or stupid."

"I bet you didn't hear that when you marched up to Jeannie that day and asked her about a seat in the van."

"Oh, I did," she told him. "But it was only a memory. You can tell memories to go away. Not like the real person."

"And it turns out, you were right," he said. "Coming on this trip was certainly not pointless. It was brave, and it turned out both *Gott* and Emily needed you right where you were."

Beth gazed at Emily, sitting on the end of the campsite's picnic table with her foot on one of the folding stools, talking to Carl across the table. As if in sympathy, he sat turned the same way, his bowl in his lap instead of on the table.

"Do you think Emily likes him?" she asked.

Seth shook his head. "Not that way. My cousin likes everybody. I think there was someone back home, but not now."

"Did she come on this trip to forget?"

"I don't think so. From what my sister tells me, it was a while ago."

"Sometimes it's hard to forget a person you care about."

He glanced at her, one brow cocked up with interest. "Is that the voice of experience?"

She made a noise of derision in her throat as she spooned up the last savory bite of the chowder. "I've never had a special friend. But I miss my grandparents. Mammi died when I was ten. Whenever I pick up a needle to repair a hem or sew a snap back on, I hear her voice. 'Every stitch matters, Bethie,' she'd say. 'Like the *Gmay*, if one goes missing, there's a hole in the fabric.'"

"What else did she say—Bethie?"

She stuck out her tongue at him. "I think Mamm got her love of quilting from her. She's the one who told me that the red square in every log cabin block represents the hearth fire. 'It has to be red, Bethie. Not orange, not yellow. Red for the fire, and for the woman at the heart of the home.'"

"She sounds like a wise woman. I didn't know that."

"Didn't know what?" Tim Eicher parked himself on the stump on Beth's other side, with his second helping of chowder.

Seth told him.

"I knew that," he said, slurping up chowder while his biscuit got soft in the bottom of the bowl. "My sister entered one in the quilt auction this year. Red square in the middle of all the cabins. Funny the *Ordnung* doesn't allow red dresses. She had to buy material just for that."

Beth nodded. "I don't think many Amish churches do. Who wants to be a living definition of 'your sins are like scarlet'?" She plucked at her burgundy skirt. "This is as close to red as most of us get. But a burgundy square in the log cabin just doesn't have the same meaning."

"You talk about quilts with this guy here?" Tim wanted to know. He scraped up the last of his chowder and sat back on the stump, finally satisfied.

Was there something unmanly about discussing the hidden

meanings in quilts? "It's one of the family businesses," she pointed out. "We could talk about shoeing horses if you'd rather. I've helped my brother when he's had too many customers in a day, and I'm sure Seth has replaced a few shoes in his time."

Tim laughed. "There was no one happier than me when your brother opened up shop. He does such a *gut* job shoeing the horses. Not even *Dat*'s work comes close."

Beth pushed away the memories of how exactly her brother had learned his skills, and the price he had paid for them. But the *gut Gott* had turned weeping into joy, and Alden had made a prosperous business for himself.

"*Mei Bruder* is thinking of taking on a partner or an apprentice," she said. "There is so much work that his days are a little more full than he likes. Mind you," she added, "every penny is welcome now, with his wedding coming up in January."

"I didn't know that," Seth said. "About him taking on someone. Is this recent?"

She nodded, feeling a little bit guilty. "Maybe I shouldn't have said anything. He was talking about it over supper just before we left."

"Then we won't bug you about it," Seth said with a *won't we?* glance at Tim. "Good for Alden. I knew he was doing well and had lots of customers, even among the *Englisch*, but not the rest of it. I'm sure we'll hear more once it's common knowledge that he's looking for help."

The conversation moved on to plans for the Grand Canyon tomorrow, and whether they'd take the train the day after that to see the scenery and visit the town of Williams. Beth noticed, though, that as people gathered around the fire to visit, Seth seemed kind of quiet.

Was he regretting their day together in the van? Having

second thoughts about moving so fast? Because she was still overwhelmed by the thrill of holding hands with him. She'd never experienced anything like it, and being that close to him for all those hours while their hands courted each other had left her ready to jump out of her skin. Or run like the wind. Or plunge into a cold river—well, maybe not that.

She'd heard other girls whispering about what it was like to kiss a young man, but nobody really talked about simply holding hands. If it was this electrifying, what would kissing be like? Ten times as wonderful? A hundred?

She wasn't sure her body could stand ten times as wonderful.

But oh, goodness, how she wanted to know for herself.

With Seth.

❧ 13 ❧

TUESDAY, SEPTEMBER 20

LORI PARKED the van near the visitor center at Grand Canyon National Park and turned to face her passengers. "Our morning is free to wander around the South Rim. Some of you will want to find a trail to take you a little ways into the canyon. You can do that, but just know that it's a lot harder coming up than going down, and you'll need twice as much water as you think. Don't miss Hopi House and the museum, and feel free to poke your noses into the lodges. The visitors' center is just over there so you can pick up a map.

"Emily, the Rim Trail is paved and pretty flat. I'm going over to the bike rental place to get us signed up for the bike tour at one o'clock. They rent wheelchairs there, and you can go all along the rim in one for as far as you want."

"I'll go with you," Janelle said.

"I will, too," Delia said. "I've lost my taste for going down into canyons, I'm afraid."

"Hopefully no one goes too deep into this one," Lori told them. "It's a mile to the bottom."

"A mile?" Jude gaped at her. "How is that possible?"

"When you get over there, one look will tell you. All right, who's up for a seven-mile bike tour?"

Beth flung up a hand, and Seth didn't hesitate. Along with them, Lori listed Jude, Tim, and the Yutzy siblings. "Jeannie and Chris?"

Jeannie shook her head. "My stomach is feeling a little off —not because of last night's chowder," she assured Jude hastily. "I think I'd rather be closer to the restrooms and take it easy."

"And I'd rather be close to you," Chris said, laying a hand on her belly.

The same thought ignited in Beth's mind as in those of the other girls, if their raised eyebrows and delighted smiles were any indication. Jeannie was in *der familye weg*! How *wunderbaar*!

Everyone but Emily and Janelle got out, and then Lori drove them farther on to find the bicycle and wheelchair rental. The rest of the group couldn't help themselves—like a herd of cattle intent on a patch of green grass, they practically galloped to the Rim Trail.

Jude Kauffman was the first to reach the edge, and came to a stop in a way that told Beth the view must be tremendous. When she reached it, she gasped.

"Now I know what she meant," Jude murmured, his eyes wide. "It's a wonder it's only a mile deep."

The canyon was painted in every color of the desert, layered in some places like a cake, the shades of red, orange, vermilion, and blue going down and down until they lost sight of details and saw only shapes. Far below she caught a glimpse of green and the Colorado River, but only a glimpse. The canyon was so far across that she could barely see the other side. *Grand* just didn't seem to do justice to something so mind-boggling that it looked eternal.

"It's so wide it looks like a picture," Seth said in a voice that sounded a little dazed. "As though reality ends about halfway across and then it flattens out."

"It's magnificent," she breathed. "Come on. Let's go to the visitors' center and get those maps."

"Are you going to hike a little way in?" Catherine asked her, after they'd learned about the geological forces *Gott* had set in motion in order to create such a marvel, and they had maps in hand with the trails clearly marked.

"Not me," Beth said with a laugh. "But I'm going to visit every single thing I can—viewpoints, museum, that Hopi place Lori said. Maybe even walk a little way with Emily and Janelle."

"Not hike?" Seth looked as though it had never occurred to him that she wouldn't. "But it's an adventure."

"You go. I'm just going to enjoy myself being a tourist."

"But Beth—"

"Come on, Miller," Tim said, rubbing his knuckles into Seth's ribs. "You're not tied to her apron strings."

"I'm not tied to anything," he retorted, sounding stung. "I just thought she'd like to see more of the canyon than this paved path."

"Come on, man, daylight's wasting. We only have a couple hours if we want to make it back for lunch and the bike tour."

Beth hadn't really expected an active man like Seth to join her on a very easy ramble along the rim. But she fought down a little flutter of disappointment that he hadn't. Mind you, he was probably just as disappointed that she didn't want to share another adventure with him.

No, that wasn't it. She did, but ... yesterday had been so intense that it had changed her. So intense that she'd even dreamed about him last night. She needed to get reacquainted with herself in this place of nearly infinite space. Find her equilibrium, like the ranger had said about the rocks when they fell.

"A rock stops when it finds its angle of repose," she'd told them. "Sometimes it only lasts for a few seconds before something gives way and it falls again. And sometimes it stays there for a century. It all depends on the support it finds and the steepness of the grade."

Beth needed to find her angle of repose.

Catherine went with her brother and the other three, leaving her with Jeannie and Chris. "Shall we make our way down to the Hopi House?" she suggested. "There are lots of viewpoints between here and there."

"All right," Jeannie said with a smile. "Sure you don't mind poking along with the old married folks?"

"The old married parents-to-be, you mean," she teased. "I'm so happy for you."

"We are, too," Chris said, taking his wife's hand. "*Liebling*, maybe we could talk to her now."

"About what?" Beth strolled with them to the nearest viewpoint, which involved a zigzag path and then a wide area with a railing, out on a point of rock.

"About the Siksika Valley," Chris said. "We've been talking it over, and the more we think about it, the more we feel *Gott* guiding us to settle there."

"Oh, I hope so!" She leaned on the rail and lifted her face to the breeze, which likely never stopped blowing down the funnel of the canyon. "I can't say for sure and certain when my mother and Willard will announce their plans, but I have a feeling it will be before Christmas. After the wedding, of course, we'd be moving out."

"Do you think your house would suit us?" Jeannie asked.

"I think so. I like it. It's smaller than some, but the east district's *Gmay* isn't so large that everyone won't fit. It has four bedrooms, one down and three up, but only one bathroom."

Jeannie laughed. "I've never had more than one bathroom in my life, and I'm number six of eight."

"Me either," Chris said. "And the property?"

"Half an acre, maybe? It's in town. But it does have an orchard in the back with *gut* apples. My sister and I are busy at harvest time, drying apples and making pies and canning applesauce. And I think your trade would be welcome, Chris."

"I've been working at a buggy maker's since I left school and got an apprenticeship there. But if that isn't needed, I can also work with harness and tack. They do go together, after all."

"Seth's cousin Joshua is a harness-maker. But we have to order buggies from Ohio—there's no buggy maker closer."

"Is that so?" Chris turned from the view, his eyes filled with more than simply a natural vista. He was looking at the future. "If I opened a shop, you think it might do well?"

"It's not my business," she said awkwardly, "but don't see why the Amish communities in Montana and maybe even Colorado wouldn't buy from you. You may need to go to the bishops—you know, we don't have our own standard for buggies out here, like they do in Lancaster County and Holmes County and Shipshewana. Just what people bring from wherever they lived before. If the bishops decide we need our own style for our own weather and roads, you could be busy for years, as buggies wear out and people have to order new ones."

"That *is gut* news," Jeannie breathed. "I wonder if maybe we should ask Lori to take us back to Mountain Home with Beth and Tim and Seth, and not go east so soon."

"You want to change our tickets?"

His wife said, "She's taking them north, and then going east to drop off the Yutzys in Amity before she goes home to Denver. We can change our tickets to get on the train there."

"Then you could collect your brother Peter," Beth offered. They resumed their walk toward the Hopi House, which was some distance away.

"That is, if he hasn't decided to stay for good." Chris chuckled. "Or he might be so saddle sore by now he's already gone."

"It would be *wunderbaar* if you could move out here," Beth said shyly. "I mean, you already have friends."

Chris grinned as he opened the door of Hopi House for his *Fraa*. "If nothing else, that confirms for me that all this might just be part of *Gott*'s plan."

After lunch

Already, Beth was regretting the impulse that made her raise her hand at Lori's suggestion that they rent bicycles for a seven-mile ride. What had she been thinking? She'd never actually *ridden* a bicycle.

In Whinburg Township, they weren't permitted by the *Ordnung*. If something with two wheels couldn't be powered by a human foot on the ground, it was not allowed. Beth wasn't certain what the difficulty had been; after all, the rules allowed the belts on generators. Why not the chains on bicycles? The two basically served the same function. However, arguing with the elders or the *Ordnung* was unthinkable, so she and Julie had shared a scooter if they needed to go to town or run an errand.

No one had been more surprised than they when Patricia King had come to a volleyball game recently with a brand new bicycle from the feed store. Even more surprising was that eventually, after some serious discussions between Little Joe and the elders, their bishop had let it be known that if a person lived three miles or more out of town and had to get to work or perform some other errand in the absence of a buggy, a bicycle would be permitted. Beth thought that Patricia's sister Clara, who had been designated Patricia's driver to get to work, was happier about the new practice even than the male *Youngie*.

Beth herself had actually dared to cross the highway to look at the bicycles, only to be informed by the proprietor that they were sold out. Just as well. Their house was so close to the old part of town, where the quilt shop and Alden's smithy were, that shank's mare did just fine.

So here she was, at the Grand Canyon with a group of *Youngie* who were all raring to go. Even Jude, who was technically still living under the *Ordnung* of Whinburg Township. But nobody was paying attention to technicalities. Out here in Arizona, there were no Amish. As Jude said, laughing, that meant it was a rule-free zone.

Maybe for him. Beth couldn't get the hang of it, *Ordnung* or not. Clearly the ability to ride a bicycle was a gift, and people like Patricia King and Tim Eicher had it. She did not. She could no more keep the wretched bicycle upright than fly to the moon, even after the rental folks tried three different sizes.

"Once you get going, it will be easy," Seth assured her. "The momentum helps you stay upright."

He and Tim were wheeling their mountain bikes around the parking lot as though they had been doing it since they were children. Mind you, riding a horse might have been practice in some ways, but she didn't do that, either. She wasn't from a ranching family, like Susanna and the Miller girls at the Circle M. They'd learned young how to help with the cattle, whereas she'd learned even younger how to help Mamm in the home.

"Ischt okay," she said, giving up when, ever sensitive to disapproval, she spotted more glances at the sun than smiles of anticipation among her friends. "You all go ahead and have a wonderful time. I'll have just as good as time with Emily and Janelle. It won't take me long to catch up to them."

Seth coasted up to her, his eyes filled with dismay. "You have to come," he protested. "Just try it one more time. If you don't go, then I won't have any fun, either."

"Yes, you will. There's no reason for you to miss out just because I'm uncoordinated. Go on, now. We don't want to keep the group waiting any longer than they already have."

"Are you sure?"

He deserved to get the most out of this trip. She would never insist on his staying behind. "Certain sure." She put all the reassurance she could into her smile, and at last he seemed to accept that they wouldn't be having this adventure together.

Not that they could, anyway. Whatever this was between them was too new and too fragile to show in public any more than they had already. On this particular subject, Seth seemed to be sensitive to teasing, and Beth couldn't blame him. Even when somebody took a girl home from singing in his buggy, the teasing was like a gauntlet he had to run, and the girl would often have to wait at the end of the driveway in the dark for him to pick her up in order to avoid it.

They set off down the road, Tim with the map of the route that the rental place had given him tucked inside his shirt.

Beth returned the third bicycle to the shop with a regretful smile and headed back along the Rim Trail to the last place she had seen Emily and the others. Pushing a wheelchair, they couldn't have gone far.

4:00 p.m.

They had agreed to meet in the parking lot at the van once the adventurers had turned in their bicycles. Beth prowled the parking lot restlessly, peering down the path toward the rental place, and then circling the parking lot in case they might be coming from a different direction.

She was anxious to hear about the tour, and to share her, Emily, and Janelle's experience of being surrounded by a herd of elk right there on the Rim Trail, and being unable to move until the grazing animals moved on.

The wind carried the sound of voices speaking *Deitsch*. "Here they are at last," Lori said, climbing out of the driver's seat.

But there were far more voices than a group of six would make. To Beth's astonishment, when they emerged from the bicycle shop into the parking lot, their little group of *Youngie* had doubled in size.

Tim Eicher waved and jogged over. "You'll never believe what happened," he said, grinning as if it were Christmas morning. "We met another group of *Youngie* on the trail, and we did the whole return trip together."

What were the chances of *that*? "Are they on a van trip ... too..." Her voice faded away to a whisper.

Because here came Seth, trailed by a young woman wearing an Ohio *Kapp* and a young man who looked so much like her he must be related. "Beth, can you believe it? Here we are, hundreds of miles from home, and who should I meet but two of the *Youngie* from our old church in New Mexico!"

The young woman smiled at Beth and offered her hand. "Seth tells me you're from Whinburg Township. I have family there, too—do you know the Kanagys?"

"*Ja,*" she said, dazzled by her friendliness and charm. "But we left a long time ago and haven't been back to visit."

"After we left New Mexico, my father inherited *Daadi*'s farm in Holmes County, so that's where we are now. I'm Phoebe Plank, and this is Joachim, one of my brothers. He said he came along to keep me out of trouble, but I think it's because he wants to find some himself."

While Seth and Joachim laughed, Beth murmured a greeting and shook his hand. The girl was so pretty it was difficult not to stare. Seth wasn't having any trouble—she couldn't tell whether the uplifted expression on his face was from staring at Phoebe, or simply from being so glad to see old friends that he couldn't help it.

She hoped it was the latter.

They were swiftly introduced to the chaperones, two other girls from Ohio, a pair of young men from Kansas, a boy from Wisconsin, and one of the *Youngie* from Amity whose name Beth had heard but whom she'd never met—Grace Ann King.

"I hear you know my cousins," Grace Ann said shyly as introductions were made to the rest of the group. "Patricia and Clara King? And Simeon and Noah?"

They must be in regular touch with each other, if Grace Ann had left out the name of the middle brother, Andrew. That didn't sound *gut*. She'd thought he'd come back to the church and was getting married out east.

"I know them well," she said. "My mother owns a quilt shop in Mountain Home, and Patricia works for her. We trade shifts. Seth probably told you she and his brother Gideon are special friends."

Grace Ann threw a frown at Seth, whose back was turned as he caught up on the news from the Planks. "He did not," she said. "And neither did Patricia. I'm half tempted to ride home with you and get all the news right from the horse's mouth. After I read him a lecture about leaving out the important stuff."

"You should," she said. "They would love to see you. Just remember, I didn't say a word about Gideon and Patricia. Or Clara and Calvin Yoder."

Grace Ann's eyes widened. "Goodness me. Clara has a special friend? Now I'm really coming to visit. I have to see this with my own eyes."

Beth laughed and allowed as how observing Clara's *gut* management of Calvin Yoder was certainly worth a visit.

Emily and Janelle joined them. "Where are you folks staying?" Emily asked Grace Ann shyly. "We're camping just outside the park."

"We are, too!" Grace Ann exclaimed. "I can't believe we didn't run into each other last night. We've been here two days already. We're heading on to Yosemite tomorrow."

"Yosemite? Isn't that in California?" Beth asked.

"Yes, but—"

"What parks have you been to?" Janelle interrupted.

Grace Ann shook her head. "We've only just started. We went to Mesa Verde first, then here, then next are Bryce Canyon and Zion. I can't wait for those—they're supposed to be beautiful. After that is Yosemite, and then out to the coast. I've never seen the Pacific Ocean, so I'm looking forward to that. Then the train home."

Emily shared the journey they'd been on, but Beth took note of the fact that she left out the adventurous parts. Time enough for that. No point in horrifying their new friend too early.

She stole a glance over at Seth, who was practically waving his hands as he talked. She'd never seen him so excited—self-controlled, laconic Seth Miller seemed overjoyed not at making new friends, but at seeing the old ones.

She squashed down the question, but it kept rising, like a bubble. Finally it popped.

Just what kind of friend had Phoebe Plank been to him?

❧ 14 ☙

BOTH GROUPS TOOK it completely for granted that they would have dinner together in camp—the only decision was whose campsite would host. Since the other group's was the largest, and set under a little copse of pines, that decision was easy. Seth walked over with Tim Eicher and Joachim Plank, each carrying some groceries to contribute to the communal meal.

"You have a trailer?" he said in some amazement when they arrived. It had been unhooked from the van so the group could travel to various places in the park. Four roomy tents formed a semicircle under the pines.

"It came with the van," Joachim said. "I don't have a lot of luggage, but my sister brought a little rolling suitcase and a backpack. I suppose she thought we'd be going to church every Sunday."

"We *have* been going to church," Seth said. "Our own. Last Sunday was on a cliff overlooking the mesas, and the Sunday before that, I think, was in Glacier."

"That was before we joined," Tim put in. "What have you got in there?"

"Mostly camp chairs, cooking stuff, and the barbecue. And the luggage."

They had a barbecue! "You must be on the luxury tour. We've been cooking on the campfire and a Coleman stove. Okay, we've got sausages in here." He peered into the grocery bag. "And potatoes."

"Food is the girls' department. Just leave them on that cook table. Phoebe and Grace Ann are in charge."

"We're paired up," Tim said. "Each of us has a partner and we take turns cooking."

"*Ja?*" Joachim looked almost puzzled. "Guys, too?"

"I don't mind the chance to learn," Seth said mildly. "When you're cowboying, it's not like you expect to eat at the big house every night. My boss now is *mei Onkel,* but it hasn't always been that way."

"Still cowboying, hey?" Joachim grinned. "Not me. If there's cows involved in any job, I turn it down. I'm working at an RV factory outside town. *Gut* wages, fair hours, and I never come home covered in calf splatter."

The evening turned a warm gold as the sun began to set. Their group walked over and soon the air was filled with chatter and the exchange of news and details of their trips. And the all-important question of who was related and who wasn't. Seth already knew he wasn't related to the Planks, but if his brother Gideon had his way, he'd soon be a shirttail relative to Grace Ann King.

Derek, the other group's driver, got the barbecue going while Lori leaned on the picnic table next to it, comparing notes about the best route to take to his group's next destination.

Beth, Seth noticed, had already fit into the place where she was most comfortable—the helper. She'd made sure that Emily had a chair and a folding camp stool to put her foot on. Janelle and the two boys from Kansas sat with Emily, talking a mile a minute. Seth watched as Beth took a suggestion from Phoebe, found a big metal bowl, and organized the ingredients for a salad.

She worked so effortlessly with Grace Ann that Phoebe took a minute to come over to where Seth lounged on the picnic table with a soda.

"I hear you're one of the cooks on your trip," she said, seating herself next to him on the bench and filching the soda from his hand. "Okay if I have a sip?"

"Take the whole thing. We just bought groceries, so there's another flat of soda back in camp."

"I don't want the whole thing. Just enough." She handed it back to him as casually as if they were at singing, and she'd just reached across the table to take a sip of his coffee. "What are you smiling at?"

"You," he said. "Just like old times."

"*Ach*, we were *Kinner* then. I don't think I was even eighteen when we left."

"Old enough to date."

With a chuckle, she said, "Just barely."

"And then off you went to Ohio to break all the hearts there."

"Not quite all," she said, straight-faced. "There are still a few holdouts."

He couldn't help laughing. "Hard to believe. Are you seriously telling me you're not spoken for yet?"

She stuck her nose in the air. "I have standards, Seth Miller. Mind you, back in the Ventana Valley, you were pretty much my standard. I think every man since has had to measure up to your yardstick."

"You've got to be kidding," he managed when he could pick his jaw up off the ground. "You never thought of me that way. Not even once."

She lifted a shoulder in a shrug. "A lot you know. You didn't look my way, either. I was too young for you." With a tilt of her head, she reconsidered. "I suppose I still am."

"Phoebe, we need you," Grace Ann called. "Can you get another pound of butter out of the cooler? We're going to rub these potatoes in butter and salt, and bake them in the barbecue."

"Ooh, yum."

She rose and went back to work, leaving Seth still trying to recover from a past that had clearly been much different for her than for him. He'd always thought of her as a kind of kid sister. She'd been a pretty girl then, but hadn't bloomed into the woman she was now. The young men in Holmes County must either be blind or they'd asked her out and she hadn't let the relationship go anywhere.

But it couldn't be for his sake. That was impossible.

Maybe it was a *gut* thing there was no time to rewrite the past. There were other *Youngie* to get to know, and then supper was served buffet style. Seth found a seat in the circle of camp chairs set up around the fire, and between its light and the twilight falling, he was just able to see his plate. He closed his eyes in a silent prayer of thanks.

The baked potatoes were perfectly done, fluffy and melting with a pat of butter inside. The sausages tasted just like the kind Mammi used to make, and there was even corn on the cob as well as the salad.

Beth took a seat on one side of him and one of the boys from Kansas sat on the other. Once they, too, had said grace, it was safe to speak. "*Gut* salad," he complimented her. "What a feast."

"Isn't it? Such simple food, but Phoebe and Grace Ann put a lot of care into it. That must be why it tastes so *gut*."

"Plus we got a workout today. I sure wish you could have come on the bike ride. Around every turn there was a new view that was more *wunderbaar* than the last."

"Some day, maybe. But we had a little adventure of our own. We were surrounded by a herd of elk! Mostly cows and last spring's calves. Emily had never seen an elk before the ones she saw in Glacier and Yellowstone. She didn't know whether to jump out of her wheelchair and try to run, or to sit still and hope they didn't think we were a threat."

"You went with option two, I hope." A spooked elk was a dangerous elk.

"Mostly we were paralyzed with fear ... and wonder. We didn't dare move for ten minutes, but seeing those majestic animals so close? I'll never forget it."

"I wouldn't, either. When I'm that close to an elk, it's usually because I've got my finger on the trigger."

Beth looked pained, and the boy from Kansas laughed.

"Before we headed out," she said, cutting her sausage in neat pieces like the rounds of a tree, "I had a little visit with Chris and Jeannie. I think they're going to come back with us to Mountain Home. They're really serious about moving."

"We could sure use a buggy maker. I might be the first in line to get one." He paused. "That is, if Gabriel Eicher hasn't decided that Peter Kauffman should stay on."

"Why would he do that?" Beth asked. "Peter is going home, isn't he?"

"I don't know. Unless Chris uses Lori's phone to call and ask him how it's going, we won't know for days yet."

"But why does it matter to you?"

He told her about Adam and Zach. "They're partners in the ranch, just like Daniel."

"Not Joshua?"

"He split his share between Malena and Rebecca, and told them to hold it for him." He lifted one shoulder. "He's not a rancher the way Reuben and the others are. He's happiest when he's surrounded by leather and punches and saddles and things. And the hay farm brings in *gut* money, especially since there's no mortgage."

"So what you're saying is that when Adam and Zach finish their houses, there may not be a job for you."

He nodded. "I had my eye on a job at the Keim or the Eicher place, but now..." His voice trailed away.

"There are other ranches. *Englisch* ones, too. You won't have trouble finding work."

"Sounds like you want me to stay," he teased.

He couldn't see much of her face beyond what was illuminated by the campfire's flames, and he remembered too late they were surrounded by people, each one a tendril on the Amish grapevine.

"I want all my friends to stay," she said at last. "I just haven't figured out a way to convince Emily and Janelle."

"My sister would love it if Emily moved to the Siksika. They're fast friends. But I don't suppose it would be very easy to tear her away from her island."

"Or from—" She stopped. "Her family."

He was pretty sure that wasn't what she had started to say, but he didn't push. Instead, some impulse made him lower his voice. "What would it take to tear you away from the valley?"

Her gaze met his and lowered to her nearly empty plate. "I

can't imagine anything that would. I'm happy there. My family is there. So is yours."

His heartbeat picked up its pace. "What if you fell for one of these guys?" His gaze moved from Jude, sitting next to Phoebe, then around the circle to the boys from Kansas and Wisconsin.

She made a rude noise and finished her corn on the cob. "Why would you even say that?"

"I don't know. I guess it was talking about having to move on to find work. All the folks here but Tim and you and I are from somewhere else."

Beth put down her corncob and gave him her full attention, her gaze searching his face. "Are you really thinking of leaving?"

"I'm not at this moment, but I may have to. A man has to eat and sleep somewhere, and cowboying ... well, you go where the work is. Just ask Luke. He can't wait to marry Mamm—not just because he loves her, but because he'll have a home for the first time since his family were—"

She nodded. He didn't need to finish.

"Don't you want a home, too?" she asked softly.

But he couldn't untangle his thoughts long enough to put them into words. He'd never given it much thought. Not until this trip, when the danger of losing not one, but two opportunities for work that would keep him in the valley seemed to be rearing up like an out-of-control bronco. And if he had to leave, where would that leave Beth? He couldn't ask a woman to tag along after him from ranch to ranch, never having a home of her own, never knowing if they'd have to move on after the cattle went to market. And what about *Kinner*? What kind of father would he be, out on the range sometimes for days at a time, leaving her alone to look after both lodgings and children?

The fact was, unless you owned land, or were hired on as foreman like Stephen Kurtz, cowboying was mostly a solitary job for single men.

Unlike Joachim Plank, cows were pretty much all Seth knew. All he'd ever wanted to know. In the early days, it hadn't occurred to him to look beyond partnering with his brothers and Dat to make a success of the ranch. But one by one, his brothers had begun to make plans that didn't include him.

Everything was changing again.

This was why he didn't get attached to things. They always changed. He hadn't had a choice but to roll with it, like a trout in a river, the current taking it to new banks and pools.

You always have a choice. You're not a trout, you're a man with the brain Gott gave you. You just have to use it on more than cows and horses and the weather.

"Seth?"

He came back to the real world with a jolt, and realized he'd never replied to her. And with everyone talking and laughing around them, it wasn't the right time for something so personal, anyway.

Out of habit, he took her plate and stacked it on his own. "What did those girls come up with for dessert? How about I go find out?"

But when he came back with several squares of store-bought fudge that either Lori or Derek had added to the bounty on the picnic table, the camp chair next to his was empty and he couldn't see Beth anywhere in the circle of firelight.

"Ooh, that looks *gut*." Phoebe Plank seated herself in Beth's chair and took one of the fudge squares off the paper plate. When she bit into it, she said, "My favorite. Maple sugar."

Seth couldn't remember the last time he'd had maple sugar fudge, so he took the other one, and passed the plate to the boy on his other side. He'd get another plate for Beth if she came back. "Mmm," he said. "Where did these come from?"

"A gift shop somewhere. I forget. Did you enjoy your supper?"

"I was pretty hungry. Those weisswurst sausages are tasty done on the barbecue."

"I was hungry, too. Seven miles of pedaling will do that to you." She sat back, licking fudge off her fingers and gazing at the fire. "I can't decide whether to have a shower tonight or in the morning."

"Tonight," Seth suggested. "If you're heading west, you probably have an early start."

"We do. I can't wait. Derek says Bryce and Zion are similar to the Grand Canyon, but completely different in a lot of ways."

"Size being one, I suppose."

She laughed. "The Grand Canyon is bigger than anything I ever saw. Except for the Pacific Ocean. We'll see that next week."

"Next week I'll be home," Seth said on a note of realization. "Back to work. Riding fence and repairing whatever needs fixing in the barn, painting the cattle pens now that they're empty. The usual autumn stuff."

"None of that is urgent. It will wait for you."

"It's been waiting for two weeks. But if a fence post gets knocked over, I expect Gideon will find it and repair it."

"Gideon is well?"

"Last I saw." At least he had some news to share. "Which isn't often. He's got a special friend these days."

"I heard. Grace Ann's cousin, *nix?*"

"*Ja*, Patricia. She works for Beth Stolzfus's mother in the quilt shop."

"Beth's *mamm* has her own business? *Gut* for her."

"It is *gut*," he agreed. "She sells quilts on consignment, as well as fabric, and makes a nice living, from what I understand. When Patricia can't come to work, Beth helps out."

"Beth seems like a helpful kind of person. Saved me from making that salad. The potatoes took longer to prepare than we thought."

"She is. In more ways than one. She's studying to be an EMT."

Phoebe stared. "Like ... in an ambulance?" In the firelight, he realized he'd forgotten how blue her eyes were—like those little alpine flowers Mamm liked. Gentians.

"We don't have an actual ambulance, but the town bought a medical van. Two of my cousins are EMTs with the volunteer fire department. They're encouraging her to get her license. There are times when a woman is needed, apparently, and she wants to do it."

"That ... seems strange to me. I've never heard of a female EMT."

"My cousin's wife is one, though she doesn't do it so much anymore now that the baby is coming. And they have them in Lancaster County."

"Don't you think it's ... forward, somehow? Unwomanly?"

She couldn't be serious. "*Neh*. If Adam and Zach say there's a need, and she feels led to do it, why shouldn't she?"

"And your bishop agrees?" Clearly to Phoebe this was the only real deciding factor.

"*Ja.*" He didn't elaborate. Why was she taking exception to Beth's choices in life? It wasn't going to affect her in any way.

Then again, Beth's choices weren't likely to affect him in the end, either. Not if he had to roam farther afield to find work.

Phoebe fell silent, contemplating the fire. Then she slouched in the camp chair a little and stretched out her legs, crossing them at the ankles. "I had a reason for saying the ranch work would wait for you."

"Oh? What's that?"

"My brother remembered that you always wanted to see California. He was telling me about some animal you carved for him once?"

Seth grinned, please Joachim had remembered the thought, if not the result. "It was supposed to be a pelican. I had a bright idea of making a Noah's ark for my niece and nephew for *Grischtdaag*, and that was the first animal I managed to finish. It looked more like a marlin, though—you know, those big fish with the pointed bill and the fin like a sail?"

She laughed. "And how did the *Kinner* like the ark?"

"I never made it. The pelican was such a mess I abandoned my whittling career and gave the thing to Joachim."

"I don't think he has it anymore. Just the memory. Anyway, when he brought it up, I had a little idea. Instead of heading home with your group, why don't you come with ours?"

Now it was his turn to stare. She didn't seem to be joking. Or teasing.

She went on, "We have two empty seats. It would be a shame to miss something you've wanted to see forever, when you're so close and have an easy means of getting there. And, may I point out, friends to see it with."

California wasn't exactly close, but it was for sure and

certain closer right now than Montana. Could *Gott* have given him this opportunity? For some reason that Seth couldn't yet see, had He prompted Phoebe to suggest it?

"Would that be okay with Derek and your chaperones?" He needed a minute to think.

"Derek would rather a seat was filled than not, and he'd give you a *gut* price since it would be a partial trip. As for Tildie and Ron, they'd be only too happy to get to know a real cowboy."

He snorted—that was taking persuasion just a little too far.

"Well, maybe not," Phoebe allowed, "but Joachim and I would sure like it. I want to know about your life since we all left New Mexico. The story could take days." She smiled at him, her sparkling eyes and heart-shaped face illuminated by the fire in a way that might bowl any other man over.

Not him, though. They were just old friends.

Old friends who shared a love of travel. He could use some extra time to figure out what he wanted to do with his life. And maybe, if *Gottes Hand* was working here, he might be led to an opportunity for work that he'd miss if he didn't go.

It was also the perfect opportunity to ease away from Beth. Because the unpleasant truth was that despite his growing feelings, he had nothing to offer her ... or any other girl. If they became special friends and this thing between them progressed to thinking about marriage, what then? He couldn't support a wife and family on a cowboy's wages. And Beth had just told him she didn't want to leave the valley. If he found a job in Colorado or even eastern Montana, would the prospect of a move overshadow her own feelings?

But what they'd shared already ... those moments of joy and awe ...

A woman like that doesn't come along every day, said Jimmy Begay's voice in the back of his mind.

Were these emotions between him and Beth real? Or was it just a temporary dream brought on by not one but two shared crises and the outside-of-normal-life bubble they were in? Should he go back to Mountain Home? Or go on to see a bit more of the world and figure out his life while he was at it?

How was a man to know which path to choose?

"I have to be back in time for my mother's wedding," he said slowly. "October fourth. Gideon and I are her intended's *Neuwesitzern*."

Phoebe waved a hand. "Not a problem. We have train tickets for September twenty-ninth. Derek will get you to whatever station you're boarding from if it isn't the same one as ours."

"I could get the Empire Builder to Libby," he said, thinking hard. "Two days travel at the most."

Could it really be that easy? Is that what *der Herr* did? *I will even make a way in the wilderness, and rivers in the desert.*

And train schedules to get him home just in time for the wedding.

15

WEDNESDAY, SEPTEMBER 21

IT HAD BEEN eight hours since Seth had gone west with Phoebe's group, and Beth still felt nauseated. It wasn't car sickness, or food poisoning, which she would almost have welcomed. Those were temporary.

It was the kind of hurt that went right to the heart, dealt by someone she had believed cared about her. The kind of hurt her father had inflicted.

Only she was pretty sure that this was worse.

Because she'd let herself care, too. Had allowed those moments she and Seth had shared together at Arches and Mesa Arch and even in the Madison River build themselves into something she'd dared to whisper to herself might be a future. She, invisible Beth Stolzfus, the one nobody noticed, had dared to invite Seth Miller into her heart and believe he might stay there.

So much for acts of courage. What a mistake.

"I don't understand it," Emily Kuepfer said for the third time. Since their departure an hour after Derek's van had pulled out with Seth in it, she'd sat next to Beth in the pair of seats in the rearmost row. She'd said it was because the swelling had gone down in her ankle enough that it was safe not to keep it elevated. But Beth felt it was the act of a friend standing in the breach so that she could grieve in private.

Despite the fact she was Seth's cousin, Beth could tell Emily was as mystified by his sudden decision as Beth herself. "How could he just go off with them like that?"

"He never said a thing last night when I came back to the campfire from the restrooms. I guess he was too busy talking to Phoebe Plank."

"I wish I'd known they were planning to ditch us." Emily glared out the window at Interstate 15. "I'd have interrupted them for sure and certain."

But Beth had a feeling it would already have been too late. Phoebe had wanted him to come, and he had gone. Some girls had that power. Beth clearly did not.

"He always wanted to see California," she said sadly. "And with an empty seat in their van, in his mind I guess it made sense."

"Well, it doesn't make sense to me. I thought you and he were ..." Emily nibbled her lip, clearly uncertain whether she might have gone too far.

"So did I," Beth said on a sigh. "But Phoebe is ..." Now it was her turn to leave a sentence hanging.

"We all know how Phoebe is." Emily crossed her arms. "What would it be like to go through life being that beautiful?"

"Real beauty comes from the inside." Which may have been true, but Beth felt like a hypocrite saying so. She didn't feel very beautiful on the inside. She felt like a howling wilderness.

"Of course it does. Which I'm sure every man in camp told

himself when she walked by." Emily sighed. "Listen to me. Why don't I just meow and lick my whiskers?"

Beth leaned against her shoulder in a brief moment of thanks for the support. "It's not her fault *Gott* gifted her with a face like that." And a willowy figure, and a sense of humor. "I just thought Seth might have appreciated ... other qualities in a woman."

"I'm sure he did, until yesterday. He can't possibly like her. I mean *like* her. The way he likes you."

Beth couldn't even find comfort in her use of the present tense. Because he'd chosen to go, and who knew when or if she'd see him again, and what mere liking could stand up to that *and* Phoebe Plank?

The hypnotic motion of the van rolling north at seventy miles an hour lulled Emily into a doze, leaving Beth to the unwelcome company of her own thoughts.

The memory played itself in her mind again as though somehow the outcome might be different this time.

"I'm heading west with the other group," he'd said to her this morning, his gym bag over his shoulder and his sleeping bag under one arm. He'd offered her his hand, same as he'd done for everyone else in their group. "Goodbye for now. See you at home."

Wordlessly, she'd shaken his hand because her brain was in complete denial and her body was operating on its own. *Shake hands. Get mouth moving. Wish him a safe journey. Wave goodbye.*

And all the while she wanted to tear his gear off him and throw her arms around his neck, preventing him from leaving her by brute force.

Their group was supposed to have gone to Williams on the train today, but when Lori brought it up after the other van had gone, it seemed as though Beth wasn't the only one who had lost their spirit. When she'd suggested they might head north again on the interstate, which would get them home by tomorrow night, everyone but Tim had raised their hand.

"Guess I should have gone with Seth," he'd said with a smile, but Beth could tell it wasn't a joke. She couldn't spare any emotion for his feelings, though. She had climbed into the van as numb as though this sick chill in her stomach had frozen her brain, her limbs, and her heart.

Why had he gone? There had to be more to it than simple convenience. That old dream of California couldn't possibly be strong enough to make him deliberately break the connection that had been growing between them.

At last her thoughts brought her to the place she hadn't wanted to go. Because here it was, staring her in the face.

He *needed* to break the connection.

There could only be two reasons for that.

Phoebe was one. It was a rare man who could resist a woman like her, and she had the added advantage of a shared past. Shared experiences and people. She had known his father, too—was one of the few people with whom he could talk about those memories. Whereas for Beth, fathers were a fraught subject best left alone.

And the other reason? They had become too close too fast, and obviously Seth was having second thoughts. The opportunity to go west with the other group must have seemed like a gift from *Himmel*. Or more, a clear indication of *Gottes wille*. There was nothing that Beth could say or do if that were the case. Nothing but accept it, let the sea of forgetfulness close over him, and return to her own life.

Her mouth trembled at the impossibility of forgetting Seth. At the betrayal of her feelings that forgetting him would mean.

She had never dreamed she could feel this much. Or hurt so much.

Could this be what love was like? Had she finally realized how much she cared *now*, when he had chosen to climb into that van and was already hundreds of miles away?

Beth Stolzfus, trust you to fall in love when there's no hope of his returning it. The story of your life.

Because it was broken now, that fragile threefold cord made of trust and joy and a shared acknowledgement of a heavenly hand at work on their behalf. Even if Seth came back on bended knee and begged her to be his special friend, how could she say yes? Because if he had walked away from her once, it would be all too easy to do it a second time. Who was she that any man should put her above everything in his life but faith?

No one. Not Beth Stolzfus, the perpetual helper. The one you could count on, but not need.

She should have known it wouldn't last. But she knew now. He might come back, but it would be the old Seth Miller, not the one who had lifted his face to *der Herr* and given thanks for a bridge to heaven in golden sunlight. Not the one who had taught her that holding hands could begin forging a bond for the future.

She was done with the future. Losing it hurt too much.

It was all she could do to exist in the present and not break down in tears, locked in a speeding van taking her back to a life that could no longer make her happy.

Sunday, September 25

Death Valley.

Seth gazed out the van's big side window at a landscape

that seemed to have been created in a blast furnace. They'd stopped for a break and when they got out to stretch, he'd gasped at the temperature—well over a hundred—and probably why there were so few signs of life. Unlike Lori, whose policy had been to let people converse about what they saw as they drove, the driver of this van wore a microphone and gave a running commentary. It had been interesting in Bryce Canyon and Zion National Parks, but Seth was getting tired of it. At this moment, he did not want to know about being below sea level with this kind of lizard and those kinds of insects and the thousand species of plants the desert supported.

He was having second thoughts about coming at all.

Sure, he'd had a great time hiking over the past couple of days, soaking in the sheer beauty of the parks and storing it up so he could tell his family what it was like. But it had been different when Beth was sharing it with him. He didn't understand why they seemed to experience things in the same ways, but now that she was gone, he missed it.

Missed her.

Ja, he missed Beth Stolzfus. Her gentle, practical spirit. Her humor. Her ability to live in a moment and remind him to live in it, too. And he missed her skills—not only in cooking, though those were pretty impressive, but in jumping in to help anyone who was hurt. Derek had a first aid kit in the trailer, but even now, four days later, Seth wasn't sure the man even knew where to locate it.

And then there was Phoebe Plank.

Every Amish man in the van was in love with her. Even Derek, who was ten years older than all of them and didn't wear a wedding ring, made sure she was the first one served at dinner, the first to step up on some viewing point to take in nature's beauty, the first to choose a seat in the van. Joachim was starting to tease her about it—out of Derek's hearing, of course.

Seth had the uncomfortable feeling that Phoebe was used to people falling in love with her. He almost wondered if her friendliness toward him was less their shared childhood and more the fact that he was the lone holdout in the van.

Of all the murkiness in his life, at least *that* much was clear. He was not in love with Phoebe. And he still didn't believe she'd been carrying a torch for him all this time, either. He hadn't heard a word from or of her during all the years since her family had moved to Ohio. Granted, in order to hear, or even to write, he and she would have had to have an understanding. But not even a card to the family at Christmas?

Neh, she was just being Phoebe, saying flirtatious things and not meaning them, just because she could get away with it.

And now here they were, in California at last, and it didn't look one bit like he'd imagined. The low point—literally, some number of feet below sea level that Derek had told them and he'd immediately forgotten. Was that why he felt so restless and thoughts of Beth plagued him? The opposite of the way he'd been in the past—restless, with thoughts of the far horizon plaguing him.

He'd give a lot to see the peaks of the mountains ringing the Siksika Valley right now.

Instead, Derek was on the microphone again. "We're heading for the town of Lone Pine, and tomorrow we head north to Bishop and across the Sierra Nevada mountains. After that, Yosemite. We'll camp outside Lone Pine tonight."

They arrived at the U.S. Forest Service campground just

before four, and when Seth got out of the van, he breathed a sigh of relief. It had to be twenty degrees cooler, and he would take scrub pines and sage any day over burned-looking rock. He and the other guys set up the tents while Grace Ann and Phoebe made dinner, which turned out to be mushroom and chicken noodle casserole baked in the barbecue, with green beans boiled with bacon and chopped onions on the side.

It was still fire season in California in September, so camp-fires were banned. But that was fine by him—even twenty degrees cooler than Death Valley, it was still plenty warm and a fire would have been unbearable.

"Let's poke around a little," Phoebe suggested when the dishes were done. "I'm not going to bed this early, and it's finally cooling off. Whew! Death Valley was like walking into an oven on bread day."

They set off down a trail that meandered around sagebrush and led in the general direction of the mountains rising in the distance.

"The Sierras sure aren't like the Rockies," he observed.

"I don't think anything is like the Rockies. You're spoiled, living in the high country."

"I bet it's warmer here in the winter, though."

"True enough. But California's no place for our folk. My father calls it the State of Unrighteousness."

"He's clearly never been to Death Valley. I've never been so thankful for unrighteous air conditioning in a van in my life."

She laughed, a sound that made him smile, too. "Me either. I wish we could hurry up. I can't wait to get out to the coast so we can see the ocean."

"Mamm would say you're wishing your life away." He wondered if his mother had noticed Beth's ability to savor a moment. He should ask her sometime.

"There's nothing wrong with looking forward to things. Are you going to swim?"

"I don't have anything to swim in."

She looked around, then leaned in as though she were telling him a secret. "I bought a bathing suit just so I could swim in the ocean." With a giggle, she went on, "Grace Ann was so shocked. It's not like a bikini or anything—it's a very modest one-piece. But the *Ordnung* where she lives doesn't allow swimming in mixed company."

"And yours does?" His eyebrows rose in disbelief.

She shrugged. "I'm not in Ohio, am I?" She sounded like Jude Kauffman.

"If you have the guts to put on a bathing suit and go swimming in the Pacific, you go right ahead. I'll probably pass."

"Oh, come on, Seth. Don't be a wet blanket. There are probably swim trunks for sale all over the place. You should get some."

What did Susanna say about that word? *Should is what other people want you to do. Will is what Gott asks you to do.* When he bent to examine the sagebrush, a rabbit popped out of it and ran like the wind for another shelter. He watched the little critter go, wondering if it had a mate or a family close by.

"Seth?"

"Hm?"

"Did you hear me? I said, you should get some swim trunks."

"I think I just said I'd pass. We swim in the Siksika River, but not usually in mixed company, and it's usually after a long, hard day of vaccinating calves or rounding up cows. No need for swim trunks with my cousins. We just toss our clothes and dive in."

"But I wanted to swim in the ocean with you. Have something to remember that you won't do with anyone else." She laughed again. "Because I can't say that about very much else, can I? Kissing, for instance."

He blinked and lost his focus on the rabbit. "What?"

The laugh was triumphant now. "Got your attention, didn't I?"

"*Ja*, but I can't imagine you need that so bad you'd be so forward about it."

"Forward about a kiss? What if I meant it?"

A flush was burning into his cheeks. "Holy smokes, Phoebe. Were you always like this?"

"Of course not. I was a shy little mouse back then. Like your special friend Beth. I'd never say boo to a goose. But then I realized there's no sin in telling the truth. It only takes courage. So here I am, out here in this sagebrush, being brave and asking you to kiss me."

"She isn't my special friend."

"*Neh*? That's not what your cousin Emily says."

His mind finally engaged, like a generator firing up. "Is that what brought this on? You want to know if it's true? Well, it's not. I've got nothing to offer her."

And even as the words came out of his mouth, he felt a sense of loss, as though he were saying goodbye to Beth all over again. The first time had been bad enough. The pain and shock in her eyes had been almost more than he could stand. He'd had to take refuge in brevity, in an almost flippant good-bye, or he would have thrown out all his newly formed resolutions to do what was best for her and stayed.

"You've got something to offer me," she said, teasing. "That kiss. Don't try and change the subject."

"Phoebe, I don't have feelings for you. Not in that way."

Her pretty blue gaze was puzzled. "Who's talking about

feelings? I just want to kiss you. I always have, right from the time I was old enough to go on *Rumspringe*. And you may have noticed that for the first time in nearly a week, we're alone."

"It isn't right." He sounded like an elder, even to himself.

"We can make it right." She moved closer until they stood only inches apart, and laid a finger on his lips, as if to keep him from speaking. "If I can't share the ocean waves with you, I'll make do with sage."

He turned his head, and her hand fell away. "They call it the Sage Sea," came out of his mouth because his brain had quit working again. Or maybe it had changed to a higher gear.

"There you go, changing the subject."

A shiver ran over him, from head to foot, though the air was still.

He didn't want to be here, a kiss away from a woman who was so beautiful she thought she could have anyone. Even him. Even someone with nothing to offer except a moment, and even that would be stolen.

He didn't want anyone standing a kiss away but Beth.

She was the one who owned his kisses now, even if she didn't know it. Even if she never forgave him for the pigheaded foolishness that had made him run away from her. A kiss was meant to be special. A promise for the future. Even for a man who didn't have one. A kiss was meant for the one a man loved.

As though Phoebe wasn't even there, he walked away, following their two sets of tracks in the dust toward the campsite.

He had to get back to Beth. To tell her he was sorry. And to ask her if there was any way she would still be his friend until he could figure out his life and be the man she deserved.

He heard a sound behind him—a call—but instead of stopping, he picked up his pace and began to run.

If this is Your Hand at work, mei Vater, let Derek be willing to drive me into Bishop to catch the bus. Right now.

172

❧ 16 ❧

THURSDAY, SEPTEMBER 22

LORI TURNBULL CALLED AHEAD to the Eicher barn and to the Wild Rose Amish Inn, which meant that the whole valley knew the moment the van was due to come around the zigzag the highway formed as it entered Mountain Home. Gabe Eicher, Tim's father, had invited Lori and the other travelers to stay at their place before they went on to Colorado the next day. Lori then had the pleasure of telling Rachel Miller than her son was somewhere in California and they hadn't heard from him or anyone in that van since they'd all said goodbye.

Beth could only imagine Rachel's feelings, especially with her and Luke's wedding so close—and Susanna and Stephen's a week after that. She hoped the two grooms had another *Neuwesitzer* each could ask to be his supporter if Seth didn't turn up.

She climbed out of the van feeling exhausted and drained. At night in camp, she'd cried herself to sleep, and during the hours and hours of driving since the Grand Canyon, she'd simply stared out the window, coming alive long enough to respond to questions about five minutes after they'd been asked.

"Liewi." Mamm had run across the highway from the quilt shop and folded her into her arms right there in Alden's little parking lot. "I am so happy you're home. Let Julie look after you, and I'll close the shop early. I'll walk our guests over, and then I can't wait to hear all about it."

Alden was next to claim his hug, and then Julie grabbed her backpack and slung an arm around her shoulders.

"You don't look as though you've had a holiday," her sister said, steering her across the bridge. "More like you've cleaned a house for church all by yourself."

"The first part was *gut,*" Beth said. "If you don't count nearly drowning twice."

Julie, having already seen she was none the worse for wear, said, "You can tell us all about it at supper. Mamm has invited that couple who chaperoned you to stay with us instead of going all the way out to Eichers'. What are their names?"

"Chris and Jeannie Kauffman. They're from Lancaster County. Lori—that's our driver—told Mamm they were interested in moving here, and were wondering about houses to rent."

"New people? And young, too. *Gut*—they can rent our house, now that it's all ready for winter. I'll look forward to meeting them properly. Right now, you look like you could use a shower and a proper meal."

"We cooked," Beth protested weakly. She felt as though she could sleep for a week. But a shower and a nap would do for a start. "I told Chris and Jeannie about renting our house. I think that's why they decided to come to Mountain Home instead of catching the train east. She's just found out she's in *der familye weg.*"

"Even better." Julie led them inside, and Beth breathed in the familiar scent of baked bread and firewood and furniture polish.

"It's so *gut* to be home," she said on a long sigh.

"I know you're tired, but I have to know—what happened to Seth Miller? Rachel came straight over to the quilt shop to see if Mamm knew any more than your driver had told her on the phone. She's a bit concerned, to put it mildly."

What happened to Seth? If they had the whole rest of the day, maybe she could tell her. But right now, Beth didn't have the strength to begin. "I'm sure he'll be home in time for the wedding."

"I certainly hope so, or it will spoil Rachel and Luke's whole day. How did it go? Between you and him, I mean. I kept trying to imagine what it would be like, locked in an enclosed space with a man you can't stand."

Their old enmity seemed to have belonged to two other people. "It went—he—" And then Beth's throat closed up and her face crumpled.

"Ach, Liebling." Julie pulled her into a hug. "Was it that bad? Why, then I'll march over there as soon as he's home and give him a piece of my mind. Nobody gets to hurt my little *Schweschder.*"

Beth felt her sister's temperature rise along with her quick temper at the very prospect. She squeezed her in an attempt at reassurance. *"Neh,* it wasn't like that. He was … *wunderbaar.* We—there was something. Between us. Something *gut.*" She gulped, and tried to swallow the tears. "And then he left me. To go with another group of *Youngie.* To California."

Silence fell around them as Julie tried to put the pieces together. "Something between you that wasn't smart remarks? You mean … you had feelings for him? Seth *Miller?*"

Miserably, Beth nodded. "He saved my life. In the river. And then we got partnered together for meals and tents. And then something just ... happened." She wiped her nose with the back of her hand. "At least, it happened for me. I thought he cared, and we held hands, and he saved my life *again* ... and then ... he left. And here I am, still trying to figure out what I did wrong." Besides not being Phoebe Plank.

But she wasn't ready to share *that* with Julie. Not with Mamm and Willard and the Kauffmans due to arrive at any moment.

"You did nothing wrong," Julie said as fiercely as though she had been there. "If he started to care and then decided California was more important to him than you, then he's *narrisch* and doesn't deserve you."

Don't call him foolish. But she didn't say it out loud. She just sniffled, picked up her backpack, and climbed the stairs to Julie's room. She usually slept in the other twin bed when visitors needed hers. Mamm had already remade her bed, and one of the wedding quilts lay on it, which she only brought out for company.

Like a faded ghost, Beth collected a fresh dress and *Kapp*, took her laundry down to the bathroom hamper, and had her shower. Afterward, clean and fresh, at least her spirits had improved enough to join everyone for dinner and fool them into thinking she was happy to be home. Well, she was. She was even more happy to let Chris and Jeannie tell her family all about the trip. Even the story of her falling in the river, and the flash flood. Beth had to reassure her mother that she was perfectly fine, and Emily's ankle was healing well.

The wounds of the body healed much more quickly than those of the heart.

When Mamm brought in the coconut snowball cake that

Willard Zook had brought with him, her face glowed. She cut pieces and Beth handed them around while Julie poured *Kaffee*. Beth could feel something in the air, something sparked by the glances that Rose and Willard exchanged.

The cake. Coconut snowball cakes were made for *weddings*. Realization broke over Beth in a wave, and she caught Alden's eye. When he nodded with the same realization, the first real happiness she'd felt in days trickled into her heart like a healing balm.

"Chris and Jeannie, I'm glad you're here to share this with us," Willard said diffidently. "Especially since what we have to say will affect you, if what I hear is so."

"Willard asked me to marry him last night," Mamm said, blushing like a girl. "And I said I would."

"Of course you did!" Beth jumped up to hug her, then ran around the table to do the same with Willard. The poor man was trembling with nerves like an aspen in a breeze. "I'm so happy." With the sincerity of her hug, she distinctly heard him sigh with relief.

Julie followed, and then Alden shook his hand as though it were a pump handle. Willard and Mamm fell back into their seats. "Whew, that was something," Willard said, hauling in a breath. "Standing up in front of the *Gmay* can't be so difficult."

"It depends on the woman you're standing up with," Chris assured him with a laugh. "Take it from me, when she's the right woman, you can't wait to say *I will*."

Jeannie took his hand and smiled into his eyes.

"Have you settled on a date?" Julie asked. "I hear Little Joe has a busy winter ahead."

"We have to meet with him and his black book," Mamm said, glancing at Willard. "But we thought maybe early

November. We don't want to delay into Christmas, and especially not later, like February or March."

At Jeannie's puzzled look, Alden explained, "That's calving season. Makes it hard for the ranch folks to come."

Chris nodded in new understanding. "So if we spoke with your landlord, and you speak with … Little Joe? Is that the bishop here?"

Willard grinned. "He's six foot seven and has a voice like the angel Gabriel's trumpet. They called him Little Joe as a scrawny kid, and seeing how much the *gut Gott* likes a joke, it kind of stuck."

Chris laughed. "In that case, once he and you folks settle on a date, then maybe Jeannie and I could arrange to rent this place in January?"

Mamm nodded, and reached over to squeeze Jeannie's hand. "I've been very happy here. I hope you will be, too. And you'll be glad to know that the windows upstairs are brand new, thanks to Abram Yoder and my intended, and we just installed a new toilet while you all were gone."

"Bliss," sighed Jeannie. "I promise I will look after it just as well as you have." She glanced at Chris. "And when it's our turn for church, I hope you'll like what you see."

"As long as the house is furnished with happiness, I know I will," Mamm assured her. Then she glanced at Beth. "My *Dochder* is falling asleep where she sits. Bethie, if you want to go up, you should. All of us understand."

But being alone in the dark—even with Julie in the other bed—was more than Beth was ready for. "It's all right, Mamm," she said, and got up to pour herself a cup of coffee. "I can sleep anytime. It's not every day I get to celebrate my mother's engagement. Who would like another piece of Willard's delicious snowball cake?"

To Seth's frustration, Derek shook his head over the subject of a bus out of Bishop being able to get him where he wanted to go soon enough. "You'd do better to go with us to Yosemite in the morning," he said. "There's an Amtrak connector bus leaves from the visitor center every day to go to the station down in the Bay Area. If you want to get home to Montana in a hurry, that's the best way to do it."

Hanging on to his patience for an evening and the night was probably the most difficult thing Seth had ever done, with the possible exception of birthing a calf in a blizzard in February. On the whole, he would rather deal with the calf, since at least with a birth, he knew when the suspense would be over.

And there would be no danger of Phoebe asking him what was wrong. Three times so far.

Finally, when it was clear she wasn't going to take running away for an answer, the next morning he invited her to sit with him in the van. As a last resort, he would tell her exactly what was in his heart.

"I didn't mean to hurt your feelings," he said, gripping his hands together in his lap and keeping his voice low. "The fact is, I have feelings for Beth, so it didn't feel right to think about kissing you."

"But you did think about it," she said softly. "I know you did."

That wasn't the way of it at all, but if she needed to believe that to satisfy some need inside he didn't understand, then he would just have to let it go. "I hope you'll forgive me. I hope we can still be friends like we always have."

But she just turned her head to look out the window, and

after the next restroom break, she chose to sit with Grace Ann. He could hear them in the front seats, laughing at some joke that was probably on him. But he simply didn't have the strength to care.

His whole heart was focused on getting home and seeing Beth. On figuring out how to explain that he had been a fool.

As the miles scrolled past and the scenery changed to granite mountains and twisted pines that had been young when Jesus walked the earth, he forced himself to look at his own behavior in a way he never had before. Without hiding. Without throwing up a joke or a smoke screen. The simple truth was, he had been a coward. A coward with the mind and reactions of a teenager, instead of a man who wanted to court the woman he loved.

Yes, loved.

He didn't know how or when it had happened. But somewhere between hauling her out of a river and seeing her kneeling next to Emily on that rock with a maelstrom roaring below them, it had. The old things had passed away, and all things became new. He needed to shed the old Seth completely now, and become a man who wasn't afraid of the future. Who wasn't afraid to change his circumstances so he could make the best life for her he could.

With a sigh, he leaned his head back on the seat. He'd been thinking like that frightened boy watching everything being taken away from him, one person and one place at a time. That boy had vowed never to get attached to anything because the pain was just too great when it was taken away.

The difficulty with that kind of thinking was that it damaged the heart. And worse, it didn't allow for Beth Stoltzfus.

Beth might be taken from him by the hand of God, but she

wouldn't leave him any other way. He knew that even though she'd never said it aloud. She would remember their wedding vows and stand by his side, no matter what.

Und glaust daß es vom Herren ist und durch dein glauben und gebet so weid gekommen bist?

And do you believe that it is because of God's will that you have come together?

Yes, he could say that without reservation. Why else would God have directed both their families to the Siksika Valley, of all the places in the country? Seth would learn to be the kind of man who would stand by her side. To be the one she could lean on instead of the one that she had to help. Because they both believed they had been drawn together in *Gottes wille*.

And if that meant searching for a future that didn't include cowboying, then maybe he should look to his brother Tobias as an example. During the dry spells, he had gone to work at the feed store, out back in the most humble position—the hay shed. He had children to provide for, and he was not about to live off their mother's goodness. He had done any job he could, out there in his buggy in all kinds of weather, delivering things as wildly different as baby trees and engine parts to the outlying ranches. Anything the customer needed, he would get it to them, even when he had to take refuge in a barn during a blizzard.

Seth gazed out the window, seeing not his brother's labor, but his love. If Tobias could do it, and be worthy of a gentle soul like Sylvia, then Seth could, too.

If he could manage to undo the damage he had done with Beth.

When they finally—*denkes, mei Vater*—reached Yosemite's visitor center, with a sense of profound relief he waved goodbye to the van bearing the group of *Youngie* and their chaperones as it pulled out of the parking lot, ready for the next adventure. And when he boarded the connector bus, he waved the thought of California away for good.

No regrets. He had work to do.

When the bus decanted him at the train station a couple of hours later, he secured a seat on the Daylight Limited, heading north. When they reached Portland, he handed over a pile of his rapidly dwindling holiday cash for a ticket on the Empire Builder.

There was just enough money left once he reached Libby for the bus to Mountain Home. Which meant his last meal had been a bag of trail mix somewhere back in California. But when it came to a choice between buying a hamburger and getting home to Beth, there was no contest. His stomach would recover, but even one day more spent figuring out a cheaper way to get to Montana was intolerable.

Wednesday, September 28

Seth got off the train at the familiar station in Libby at ten past five in the morning. *And the evening and the morning was the third day.* The third day of his odyssey, by which time he was a little loopy from exhaustion and existing on crackers other people had left on their tables. Normally someone would have called Jimmy to pick him up, and he'd see their *Englisch* friend yawning in his white taxi-van and nursing a cup of coffee that had to be a foot tall. But Seth didn't have a cell phone, and places didn't have pay phones these days, so no one knew he was coming.

It was a strange, lonely feeling to think that not a soul except the clerk at the ticket window in Portland knew where he was. In his normal life, he was surrounded by family, whether at work at the Circle M or at home at the Wild Rose Amish Inn. He simply couldn't remember when he had ever been so starkly alone—not on a mountainside during roundup, not riding fence, not walking down one of the country roads in the valley to run an errand. Because in the valley, while you might be alone, you were never far from a friend. Never lonely. Never conscious, as he was now, that if something happened to him, it would be a very long time before Beth would know. Or his family, for that matter.

He'd best make sure no further adventures happened to him.

He walked over to the closed bus station and sat on the bench outside, trying to ignore his gnawing stomach. The station opened at seven and he was the first in line to buy a ticket to Mountain Home.

The only person in line, or in the station, for that matter, except the clerk, who raised an eyebrow through the ticket window. "Bus doesn't go until nine, son."

"I know." The first time he had spoken aloud since Portland. He cleared his throat. "I hope there's a seat on it for me."

"Lucky you're first. Them quilters usually fill the extra seats with their bags."

The quilters' bus. He had to smile. He'd be in *gut* company, at least.

The quilters began arriving at eight, and by the time twenty women and all their tote bags and food boarded the bus, Seth could barely find a place to sit.

"This Amish boy is coming with us!" one exclaimed happily. "Young man, what's your name?"

"Seth Miller," he said.

"Miller!" exclaimed another. "Any relation to the quilt designer Malena Miller?"

"She's my cousin. I work for her father."

Amid the excited babble, he was able to pick out the fact that Malena was giving a quilt class that day at Rose's shop, hence the unusually large numbers of bags.

"Girls, we're going to need space in these bags for fabric. Who's for breakfast? Seth, would you like some of this?"

Would he ever. Breakfast turned into a kind of traveling buffet, and the ladies, who ranged from twenty to eighty, made certain that he wouldn't get off the bus with an empty stomach. It was almost like being with the women of his own family. Maybe quilting and food and the care of stray lambs went together, no matter whether you were Amish or *Englisch*.

In any case, when he finally disembarked, bade them all farewell, and wished them a good day with Rose and Malena, he watched them straggle across the highway from the bus station in a big, excited bunch, making sure the oldest didn't fall behind. Lucky thing there wasn't much traffic.

With a smile and a wave, he hefted his backpack and his sleeping bag and took the shortcut through the parking lot of Yoder's Variety Store and then through the belt of pines between it and the green slopes that led from the barn up to the Inn. By the time he got halfway up the slope, he was jogging.

He couldn't wait to see his family. And then he'd go find Beth.

❧ 17 ❧

SETH HAD BARELY SAID hello to the chickens dust bathing in the flowerbed when the back door burst open.

"*Seth!*" Mamm grabbed him in a hug so hard he dropped both pack and sleeping bag on the grass. His hat fell off. Two of the chickens dove under the low deck. "*Ach, Liebling.* You're home—I'm so glad. Where have you been? The other van is long gone and all the driver knew was that you were heading to California. What happened to you? Why are you on foot?"

"I'm all right, Mamm." Her *Kapp* was warm against his cheek. "I made a mistake, that's all. I got the train from California to Libby, and was lucky enough to be on the quilters' bus. They're taking a class from Malena today, apparently."

She allowed him to step back just enough to look him over from head to foot. "*Ja*, and she's in fits of nerves about it, too. *Kumm mit, mei Sohn.* Have you had anything to eat?"

He collected his hat from a salvia bush and dusted it off. "The quilters and I did nothing but eat and talk for forty miles. But it was a fair exchange—I taught them some *Deitsch* words and they fed me."

In the kitchen, she poured them both a cup of coffee, with a generous dollop of cream in hers. "I still don't know what is going on with you," she said. "When the driver called to tell me you'd gone away with some other group, I didn't know what to think. I couldn't imagine you doing such a thing. Not with the wedding so close."

"I know. I'll make it up to you—wait, you're still having it here, aren't you?" The kitchen looked just the same, smelling of coffee and the rolls she would have baked earlier for her guests' breakfast. Either the cooking was happening elsewhere, or the weekend was going to be very busy.

"*Ja*, of course. This is our home—and will be Luke's too, after Tuesday. We'll have church upstairs in the barn. You got home just in time. The work frolic is tomorrow, and the bench wagon comes Monday afternoon. Susanna and Naomi and the girls and I have been doing all the baking and cooking at Zooks' to keep the chaos to a minimum in front of the guests."

The image made him smile. Willard and Zeke would be in their element. He had a feeling it had been a long time since there had last been wedding preparations in that old farmhouse. Maybe the next time wouldn't be so long.

Her gaze didn't leave his face, as though she was making certain he hadn't changed in some way. "You still haven't told me what's going on. When I asked Beth and Tim if they knew why you'd gone with the others, they didn't have very satisfactory answers."

He couldn't stop himself. "What did Beth say?"

"Only that you'd always wanted to see California, and the invitation was too *gut* to pass up." She took a sip of her coffee and regarded him over the rim of her mug. "I didn't know you wanted to see California."

There was no getting out of it. At the same time, the

thought of confiding in her was too tempting to resist. It would be such a relief.

"I knew it was a mistake by the time we got to Death Valley," he confessed, gazing into his own mug. "And then Phoebe..."

"Tim mentioned a Phoebe," Mamm prompted after a moment. "Phoebe Plank, from the Ventana Valley?" When he nodded, she said, "I thought they moved to Ohio."

"They did. At first it was *wunderbaar* meeting someone I knew. We had lots to catch up on. And she's certainly grown up to be ... well, she's probably the most beautiful girl I've ever seen."

"Beauty comes from the inside, I've always thought."

"*Ja*, that it does. And—well, she said she'd always thought of me ... fondly."

"I see."

He was pretty sure she did. "The problem was, I made a discovery." When his mother said nothing, he realized he no longer wanted to keep it to himself. "I have feelings for Beth Stolzfus."

Mamm absorbed it, nodding slowly, as though pieces were fitting together in her mind. "I wondered."

"You did?"

"If there was something. You were always needling her. Trying to get her attention."

He wished he could send the boy he had been to the woodshed. "Maybe I was. I behaved like a child. And then on the trip, something happened. She isn't a child, Mamm. She's strong, and compassionate—and you should have seen her, quietly wrapping Emily Kuepfer's ankle while I stood there on a rock praying that I'd be taken to *Himmel* while a flash flood raged not six feet below us." He shook his head at himself.

"Nothing wrong with praying in such a place. I heard you did your share, carrying your cousin up a cliff." When he looked up, surprised, she said, "Emily told us the whole story. She's staying in the twins' old room. But when she got to the part about you going off with the other group ... she didn't say a word about Phoebe Plank."

He would have to thank her for that mercy. "Anyway, Phoebe ... well, I think she's used to male attention. And when she didn't get it from her old friend, she got a little forward. By then I was missing Beth pretty bad, and the thought of anyone else in her place just made me kind of sick."

"Like Joseph and Potiphar's wife?"

He made a face and lifted one shoulder. "Not quite as bad as that, but I certainly understand Joseph's urge to run. So I did—all the way home, on buses and trains. I had just enough cash to pay for the last ticket from Libby. Not enough for food. But I was lucky—it was the quilters' bus. They could have fed a bunkhouse full of cowboys with everything they packed along." He paused thoughtfully. "Honestly, Mamm, for the whole trip, it felt like *Gott* was working on me. Teaching me to see differently. To see myself as I really was—a frightened boy—when Beth deserves a man whose faith is strong enough that he can walk into the future with her, no matter what it holds."

"Perfect love casteth out fear," she murmured. "Your father used to say that. But ... why were you frightened?"

He reached across the corner of the table and took her hand. "Don't take this the wrong way." When she stiffened, he went on quickly, "I see now that it wasn't you. But the boy I was could only see loss. Dat. The ranch. The future I thought I had lost because you sold it. And with my cousins and brothers settling down, I saw loss again. My job. Maybe a home here, if I had to leave." He squeezed her hand and sat back, picking up his mug. "In the end, I thought that if I had nothing to offer Beth, it was better to break it off before either of us got in any deeper. So when we met Phoebe's group and she suggested I go with them, it seemed like *Gottes wille*."

"And then it didn't?"

He huffed a laugh. "Turns out it was Seth's *wille*, the big coward. He was running away before Beth decided he was poor husband material and told him to get lost."

"Poor Seth." Mamm's eyes were soft with compassion. "But yet ... you just told me you've been running toward her, not away."

"I hope I can convince her of that." His mouth quivered. "I hurt her. I'm ashamed to think of it. Worse, I don't know how to fix it, Mamm."

"If she cares, *Liebling*, you'll find a way. Would it help if I paired you up on Tuesday?"

Why hadn't he thought of that? His spirits rose just a little. "That would help a lot. And while you're at it, if they're still here, why don't you put Jude Kauffman with Sharon Keim?"

She blinked. "Oh, you haven't heard."

"I've only been home half an hour, and I haven't talked to anyone but you. Have the Kauffmans gone?"

"One of them has. The dark-haired one—Jude. With the Yutzys, to Colorado. The married couple are staying with Rose. And that other young man—the brother. Peter. He's still here."

"He's the one who wanted to be a cowboy. How did he do?"

"I don't know about that—you'd have to ask Gabe Eicher. But as a young man, he did just fine. Susanna tells me he and Sharon are courting."

Seth's eyebrows went up in surprise. "We were only gone two weeks!"

"And some women chase a man so hard it's all he can do to catch her."

Seth rocked back in his chair and let out his first real laugh in days. Maybe it was a sign. If Peter could do it, then so could he. Everyone knew that weddings made a person think about courtship.

The kitchen door opened.

Beth, carrying a stack of tablecloths, came in and stopped as suddenly as if she'd walked into a wall.

SETH LUNGED TO CATCH THE LINENS BEFORE THEY LANDED in a heap on the floor. "Hallo."

He almost sounded glad to see her. Which meant nothing. "What are you doing here?" she blurted. "I thought you were in California."

"Not since Monday. I got on the bus as soon as we reached Yosemite."

"Not beautiful enough for you?" She regretted her biting tone the minute the words left her mouth. But she couldn't help it. It was as though her body had no control over her wounded spirit—and the words just attacked.

"I'm sure it was. I was so impatient to get to the bus I didn't take in very much."

Instead of standing there trying to figure this out, she took the linens into the sitting room and put them on the sofa. "Rachel, they have one more stack over at Yoders'. I'll be back in a minute."

"Beth—"

She slid past him to the kitchen door like a fish evading a net, and headed around the corner of the verandah at a fast walk. She broke into a run down the slope.

"Beth, wait!" he called from the back door.

But when she threw a glance over her shoulder, he wasn't chasing her. *Gut*. She wasn't interested in anything he had to say. Maybe she'd never know why he was here and not a thousand miles away, but it didn't matter. The point was, he'd left her. In Phoebe's company. After that blow to her heart, changing his mind and coming back was a case of too little, too late.

At Yoders', she talked one of the girls into taking the table linens they'd collected up to the Inn, and instead of going home, decided to check whether Mamm needed any help in the quilt shop. She'd be seen all too easily from the Inn's windows as she approached the bridge, and she didn't have the strength to run away a second time. She'd probably fall into his arms and be right back where she started.

Only this time, she'd know that a blow could come at any moment.

She couldn't live like that. Not trusting him. Always expecting to be hurt in small ways and large. Just as she had with her father.

But oh, that laugh! How she'd missed it. What had prompted it, there in the kitchen having a heart-to-heart with his mother? She hoped Rachel would never know about her foolishness in falling for her son. She didn't think she would be able to stand the look of pity in those kind eyes.

The quilt shop was buzzing like a hive of bees when she pushed open the door. The quilters' bus had come in an hour ago—the bus! Had he been on the bus? He must have been. But all the way from California? Traveling for days?

What was he thinking?

Behind the cutting counter, her mother gasped at the sight of her. "Oh, Bethie, thank goodness. Can you take over the till? Patricia and I are going completely crazy in here."

As she hurried behind the till and Patricia ran to the other cutting counter, she could hear Malena Miller in the back room, which had been cleared for this special occasion. It sounded like she was telling the quilters about what had inspired a certain quilt. And more, how she translated the sight of a flower or a snowstorm into a design. Meanwhile, here in the fabric section, it seemed half a busload of women were wandering the aisles, choosing fabrics and kits, waiting in line at both cutting counters, and now surging toward the till with their cut fabric and other treasures.

Mamm needed to invest in shopping baskets. They'd be finding empty bobbins and packets of sewing needles under the stacks for the rest of the week.

An afternoon of methodically ringing up purchase after purchase was normal for the days the quilters' bus came. But today was even busier—and Beth was pathetically grateful for it. She literally had no time to think about anything except addition and subtraction, county tax, and hunting under the stacks to find the missing items the customer was sure she had picked up, but had almost certainly dropped.

At home that evening, Mamm went to bed right after supper while Beth and Julie did the dishes. Alden had taken Malena home, worn out from her first time speaking in public. And Chris and Jeannie had borrowed the family buggy to visit the bishop.

Alone with her sister, neither of them spoke much, until Julie said, "I hear Seth Miller came home today."

"*Ja*, on the quilters' bus. I saw him at the Inn when I dropped off the tablecloths."

"And ...?"

Beth shrugged. "And nothing. He said hello, I said what are you doing here, he said he came home early."

"Both of us know there has to be way more to the story than that."

"There probably is, but it doesn't matter to me." Maybe he and Phoebe had had a fight. Not that she cared.

Silence fell, in which Beth dried the pots as though her reputation depended on it.

"Won't you give him a chance to tell you?"

Carefully, Beth laid the pot and the towel on the counter and took a deep breath. "Would you give our father another chance to hurt you?"

"Seth Miller isn't our father."

"But it's the same thing. He hurt me so bad I don't know if I can ever get over it. I loved him, Julie. And he climbed into that van with another girl like it meant nothing."

"Maybe it wasn't about that girl. Maybe he had something else going on he had to work through."

"Then why didn't he talk to me about it?"

Her sister snorted. "Because he's a man?"

Even this hurt. Seth was not like any other man on the planet, and it wasn't fair that Julie could lump him in with the likes of Calvin Yoder and Jude Kauffman.

"It's done, *Schweschder*," she said quietly. "He walked away, and I can see through a grindstone when there's a hole in it."

"All right," Julie said mildly. "But it would be a shame to miss out on the man *Gott* directed you to because he made a mistake. We all make them."

But Beth was not about to argue. She'd said her piece and that was the end of it.

She might have closed the subject, but over the next two days, Julie's words came back to haunt her. What if it really was *Gottes wille* that she and Seth had both come to the Siksika Valley? Granted, it had been their mothers' decision, not theirs, but the result was the same. Was she being disobedient to turn her back on Seth Miller?

Or was something else, something more personal and insidious, going on in her heart?

Unforgiveness.

Neh. Neh, that wasn't it at all. Protectiveness was not the same as unforgiveness. A person could protect her heart and still be within the will of God. It wasn't disobedient. She would pray that *der Herr* would speak to her and reveal His will. Just because one door had closed didn't mean He didn't have an infinite series of doors for her to open.

She had to keep her faith in her heavenly Father, even if she didn't have much trust in His earthly creation. Especially that particular long-legged, laconic creation.

Saturday, October 1

"You've got a letter," Julie said, coming in after supper with the mail. They'd been so busy helping with the work frolic at the Inn and then trying to calm themselves and prepare for New Birth Sunday tomorrow that they'd both forgotten all about it.

She took it upstairs and lit a lamp in their room. The return address was some motel in Santa Cruz, California. Puzzled, she turned it over to see a loopy scrawl on the back flap. *P. Plank, Box 656, Casper Creek, Ohio.*

This had to be a mistake. She checked the front. No, it was addressed to her, care of the Wild Rose Amish Inn. Someone must have walked it over.

Dear Beth,

By now you will have been home for a few days. I hope your trip was as good as ours has been. Seth left this morning, and since this hotel has its own stationery, I thought I would write to clear something up.

I confess that I thought he came with us because he had feelings for me. I've always thought he was a man among men, and he proved me right. But when we went for a walk one evening he made it very clear that he wasn't chasing me so much as he was running away from you.

Beth gasped at the stab of pain that arrowed through her entire body. She laid the letter down while tears welled up in her eyes. At the bottom of the sheet, the words *running away from you* blurred and ran in her vision.

She couldn't bear it. He wasn't even here and he could still hurt her. She threw the letter away from her the way she would knock a spider off the wall, and dusted the contagion of it off her hands.

She heard Julie brushing her teeth downstairs, and when her sister came in a minute later, Beth had curled up on the bed, still fully dressed, her face to the wall.

"Bethie?"

But she didn't answer. She couldn't. She was crying and struggling to breathe—speech was too much to expect.

"Beth, what's this on the floor?" Paper crackled.

"Throw it in the trash," she croaked.

"Can I read it?"

Why not? Then at least Julie would understand, and leave her alone. *"Ja."*

But being Julie, she read it aloud. Beth covered her ears with her hands, but it did no good.

> *... he was running away from you. Or maybe I should say, running away from his feelings for you. But he's not running away now. There are two buses and two trains and at least three days of travel ahead of him, and I wish him well when he gets back to you.*
>
> *Your sister in Christ,*
>
> *Phoebe*

$¾$ 18 $¾$

TUESDAY, OCTOBER 4

8:30 a.m.

Rachel Miller and Luke Hertzler's wedding day

SETH AND GIDEON MILLER sat on either side of Luke Hertzler, facing Mamm. Susanna sat on her right, with Sylvia Keim Miller on her left. The preacher had told them about the marriages of the fathers, from Jacob to Joseph to the wedding at Cana. Now, as the last notes of the wedding hymn died away, Little Joe walked over to take his place between the two sets of chairs. At that moment, the sun mounted the sky enough to clear the mountain peaks and shine in the big window on the east side, just the way Noah King had designed it to do. The light fell on the *Gmay*, on Luke's bowed head, and on Mamm's white *Kapp* and her organdy cape and apron.

Seth's heart swelled. What a beautiful moment to bless his mother's union with the man who had come so far and endured so much for her sake.

He and Luke had had a little talk last night on the way back to the Zook farmhouse for the last night Luke would spend there. When they'd reached the house, Seth saw the wedding cake taking pride of place on the kitchen table before Hezekiah carefully boxed it for the trip over to the Inn in the morning. They all got to talking about Seth's trip, and then Seth found himself confiding in three single men old enough to be his father—something he'd never expected.

"I haven't seen her since the day I got back," he'd said miserably. "Part of it is the work frolic took two days and when she came over to help in the house, I couldn't get away from the barn long enough to find her. And even when I did, she'd disappeared. When I walked over to their house, she had gone to run an errand somewhere else. I never saw a girl so good at disappearing."

Willard was chewing his lips in an effort not to smile. Finally he said, "I think you might try harder. Seems she got a letter from that girl you left with. Might have changed the situation."

A bolt of fear had struck him then, like lightning blasting a defenseless tree. Phoebe had written to Beth? How did she even know the address to send such a letter to? Never mind that, what had she said that now Beth couldn't even stand his company?

All day yesterday he'd been torn between two imperatives —his mother's wedding preparations and finding out how much damage Phoebe had done. But only a child would take his own way and chase after the moon when his mother needed him. So he'd sacrificed the urge to find Beth and attempt to mend the rift—the chasm—the Grand Canyon-sized separation between them—on the altar of love. His mother deserved the full attention of all her children, and if he hadn't come to that conclusion himself, Susanna would certainly have made sure he did.

So here he was, gazing at Mamm and the man who would shortly become his stepfather, aware that among the *Gmay* in the sunlit upper room of the barn, sitting with the single women, was Beth Stolzfus. At least they were in the same room together. That was a start.

Little Joe Wengerd took a deep breath. "We have here a man and a woman who have agreed to enter the state of matrimony—Luke Hertzler and Rachel Miller. If any here has an objection to the marriage, he now has opportunity to make it known." In the silence, Seth clearly heard one of Mamm's hens celebrating an egg in the coop up the slope, on the far side of the house. The bishop turned his attention to the bridal couple. "If no one has any objection, and if you are still minded the same, you may now come forth in the name of the Lord."

Mamm and Luke rose and took each other's hands.

Little Joe spoke to Luke. "Can you confess, *Bruder*, that you accept this our sister as your wife, and that you will not leave her until death separates you?"

"*Ja*, I can," Luke said firmly.

"And do you believe that this is from the Lord and that you have come so far by faith and prayer?"

"I do."

When Little Joe asked her the same questions, Mamm's voice trembled, but Seth knew that her promise was every bit as firm.

The beautiful words of the wedding service rolled over him like a blessing. Like a promise that some day he would stand in this very place with Beth, and say them to her.

"Do you solemnly promise one another," Little Joe said, doing his best to keep his booming voice at a personal level, yet one that could be heard by everyone in the room, "that you will love and bear and be patient with each other and shall not separate from each other until *lieber Gott* shall part you from each other through death?"

"*Ja*, I promise," Luke said, gazing into Mamm's eyes.

Seth found his own lips trembling at the love and humility in his mother's face as she looked up at Luke and made her own promise. His mother, so strong, so hardworking and decisive, glowed with the softness that came with heart-deep happiness and confidence in the rightness of *Gott*'s choice for her. Maybe that was the key to her strength, he thought in a fresh glimpse of insight. Maybe that was the key to Beth's strength, too. And maybe he ought to learn a little of it from these two women who were so important to him.

"The God of Abraham, the God of Isaac, and the God of Jacob be with you together and lay His rich blessing upon you and be merciful to you," Little Joe boomed, his own happiness adding volume to the words no matter how he tried to control it. "I wish you the blessings of God for a good beginning and a steadfast middle and a faithful ending, in and through the name of Jesus Christ." Both Mamm and Luke bent their knees in respect for the holy name. "Amen. Go forth in the name of the Lord. You are now man and wife."

There were no fathers to add a blessing, but as Mamm and Luke took their seats once more, Reuben Miller rose to offer a prayer for their marriage, and that their home at the Inn would be a place of refuge not only for the traveler, but for the Holy Spirit.

When Seth raised his head, tears trickled down his mother's cheeks. No one in the valley doubted Reuben's happiness for Mamm, who had been his late brother's wife. But the fact that he chose to raise his voice in prayer for her added a special kind of blessing as she embarked on a new life with her second husband.

And then Tobias, as her eldest son, lifted up his voice as well, asking *der Herr* to bless the couple and to keep them safe no matter the storms that life might send their way. When he concluded, Little Joe announced the final hymn, the one that signified the end of every Amish wedding Seth had ever been to.

Later, as the congregation crowded around Luke and Mamm to shake hands and offer congratulations, bearing them off toward the stairs, Luke, Tobias, Gideon and even little Benny got busy with several of the young men, turning the benches and setting up the tables. His cousins from the Circle M set up the *Eck*, the L-shaped corner tables where the bride and groom and the wedding party would sit.

Mamm had not thought that a mature bride should worry about things like wedding colors and printed napkins and such, but Willard and Susanna had had other ideas. So while Hezekiah unboxed the wedding cake and set it up on its own table, Susanna and Sylvia laid white tablecloths and Mamm's best china with its painted sprays of lavender in the *Eck*, accented by Michaelmas daisies from the Zook garden in white bud vases between each place. On either side of the wedding cake on its lavender cloth were the first of the other wedding cakes—two of Willard's snowball coconut cakes, and two sent by special express from their cousin Carrie Miller in Whinburg Township, who had a reputation throughout the township for the beauty of her cakes. These ones had a spray of lavender and Michaelmas daisies made of frosting so delicate they almost looked real.

"I'm sorry we have to cut into them," Susanna whispered as she passed him with the empty cake boxes. "I've never seen anything so pretty."

"Find someone with a camera in their phone," he whispered back. "Then at least you'll have a picture to give the baker."

She laughed at his male ignorance. "The baker already knows what we want. Willard is going to make our wedding cake on Friday, and put it in the dairy to keep it cool. Only a week to go."

"It will be as *wunderbaar* as this one," he assured her.

"Don't be the odd man out," she teased, shaking her head at him. "Mamm ... Gideon ... me ... we've found the ones *Gott* wants for us." Then she sobered, and held his gaze. "Whatever went wrong between you and Beth, today would be a *gut* day to make it right."

If only it were that easy.

He had his *Neuwesitzer* duties to perform, which meant that he was trapped in the *Eck*, looking out over the *Gmay* as they tucked into the chicken *roascht*, the celery, the potatoes and gravy, the hot sliced elk roasts prepared at the Circle M, and the harvest bounty that the land had yielded up before the storms of winter descended on them. Added to that were dozens of loaves of bread, sliced and placed along the rows of tables, and pickles and salads, all contributed by the families in the valley.

He located Beth in seconds, near the tables occupied by his relatives, since her brother Alden and his cousin Malena were going to connect the two families in January. With the Stolz-fuses were Willard and Hezekiah Zook and also Chris and Jeannie Kauffman. What a way for the young couple to meet the members of their future church, Seth thought. All together like this, members of both districts crammed into the barn's upper room. It would be a wonder if the newcomers could keep any of the names straight.

After lunch, they would cut the wedding cake, and after

that the singing would begin—a tradition in the valley where the *Youngie* would sing selections from the green hymnbook and others, as well as one of the wedding hymns from the *Ausbund*. It was a tradition Seth liked—and he'd join them—but not until he'd had a chance to mingle a little and stretch his legs after being so much in view in the *Eck*.

He found his brother Gideon just outside, talking with Chris and Jeannie.

"They haven't cut the cake yet, have they?" Gid said, looking alarmed as he walked up.

"Relax. Not yet. I came out for some air."

"Me, too. I was just talking with our new neighbors."

New? "It's settled, then?" Seth asked Chris. "You're definitely moving to the valley?"

"The Lord has made the crooked way straight," he said with a laugh. "We spoke with the bishop the other night, and he'd welcome another family in the east district."

"Not only that, Rose Stolzfus was asked a certain important question a few days ago," Jeannie said with a twinkle in her eyes. "So she will be moving." She took Chris's arm and smiled up at him. "We might just be welcoming our *Boppli* into our new home instead of our old one."

"*Der Herr* certainly seems to be taking a hand in this," Chris said, shaking his head in the way people did when they saw nature at work, or acts of human love or courage. Or, in this case, a homely little miracle all their own. "I suppose it would be presumptuous to hope that a workshop might just happen to come available by then at a reasonable rent."

"A workshop?" Seth asked. "For making buggies, *ja?*"

Chris nodded. "I feel we've come where we're needed. I'd start with repairs, but once I establish myself I'd be ordering in the fiberglass bodies and building buggies from scratch. When we were talking with Little Joe—"

"I'm never going to get used to calling him that," Jeannie said.

"Me, either," her husband admitted. "Anyway, he said that he would convene the elders and then write to the other Montana bishops about gradually creating a standard appearance for our buggies. I'm to give him some sketches he can send out."

"Something that has a bit of clearance over snow and mud, and can endure the cold," Seth suggested, a little diffidently. This was the man's training, after all. Seth didn't really have much call to be advising him, but the idea of a whole new trade in the valley was exciting. "Maybe even incorporate some insulation."

"Insulation," Chris repeated. "Now you're talking change."

"A design for Montana buggies means change by default, *nix?*" he said lightly. "Insulation might make them heavier, but not by much. You could adjust for that in some other area. The seating, maybe."

Chris gazed at him. "And you said you were only a cowboy."

Gideon laughed. "None of us is really *only* a cowboy. We have to know a little bit of everything, from inoculating a calf to building a barn to repairing a pump. *Mei Bruder* is good with his hands, though. He was always the one jumping into the irrigation ditches to unstick the water gates, and suggesting a better way to build them so they didn't stick."

"I go in because irrigation ditches are cool in the summer," Seth said.

"Well, if you get tired of cowboying, maybe you'd like to come work with me," Chris said with a laugh. "I'm always open to suggestions for improvements to the buggy-making process."

An idea sparked in Seth's mind. "Wait—Gideon—what about Joshua's barn? He and Sara have the new one for the haying equipment and the buggies, but the old one is still good and sound. He has his tack and harness shop in part of it, but the rest is just waiting for a *gut* idea."

"It would be a bit of a ride to work for Chris from town," Gideon said doubtfully. "Four miles, probably."

"But it would be a start, and with the baby coming, Josh probably wouldn't turn down a reasonable rent."

"Which one is Josh?" Chris asked, looking over the folks who were outside.

"Our cousin, Joshua Miller." Gideon pointed him out. "Wouldn't hurt to talk it over. *Kumm mit*, I'll introduce you."

Chris looked over his shoulder at Seth as he walked away. "I meant it, Seth," he said. "Anytime you want to quit cowboying, come look me up. I like your ideas."

The crooked shall be made straight, and the rough places plain.

Der Herr, it seemed, was not simply concerned with bringing a new couple to the valley. Could it be he was also working to smooth out the rough places that had been holding Seth trapped like a cow in an arroyo? He felt almost breathless at the magnitude of such mercy and love.

Denki, mei Vater, for looking down at such an insignificant person as me, and helping me to see what a crooked maze I was making of my life. I thank Thee for opening this door that I didn't even know was there. If this truly is Thy will for me, help me to listen carefully and walk circumspectly. I believe that Beth is the one Thou hast chosen for me. Help me not to let anything get in the way of Thy will. Especially myself.

He could barely contain himself, but he couldn't very well

gallop upstairs and interrupt Beth in the middle of helping to clean up after the wedding lunch. He had to school himself to patience. The singing helped to calm him, with the advantage of being able to steal glimpses of her down at the end of the next table. After the bride and groom's visits to each table to distribute cut pieces of wedding cake and thank people for sharing the day with them, the older folks gradually made their way home.

Two hours later, Seth's moment was upon him. Time to pair off for dinner.

Gideon, as the senior of Mamm's two *Neuwesitzern*, stood at the top of the stairs, with the *Youngie* ranged along the steps and pooling at the bottom. Of course he'd pair himself with Patricia King. But would Mamm have remembered her promise? Especially since Beth was here at the bottom of the steps, too, pretty much as far as she could get from him without actually going out the door?

His mother wouldn't forget. Not while *der Herr*'s mighty hand was still in charge.

"Peter Kauffman and Sharon Keim," Gideon announced.

With a giggle, Sharon gave Peter her hand and they climbed the stairs together. Usually the *Youngie* waited upstairs in the bride's house, boys in one bedroom and girls in another, and came *down* the stairs. But this wasn't your everyday wedding, what with paying guests in the Inn who had to be considered. And why had he never noticed before how much Sharon giggled? He hoped Peter liked the sound—he could be hearing it a lot.

"Calvin Yoder and Clara King."

Calvin tripped and fell up the stairs. Clara gripped the railing and steadied him, and they made it to the top without further incident. Seth did his best to calm his jumping stomach.

"Emily Kuepfer and Tim Eicher." As Tim helped her up the stairs, only limping a little now, Gideon caught Seth's eye. "Seth Miller and Beth Stolzfus."

Denkes, Mamm. And Gideon, for understanding how much this meant to him. And *der Herr,* for caring about the smallest details of His plan.

Beth didn't move for a full two seconds, as though she had been frozen with horror. Then she lifted her chin, made her way through the crowd, and allowed him to take her hand. He dared to give it a squeeze as they climbed the steps together, but she didn't squeeze back.

All right, then. He had some work to do. But he couldn't help but feel that all the heavy lifting had already been done.

BETH COULD BARELY BREATHE.

She'd known this was going to be difficult, but her worst imaginings had *not* included that squeeze of her hand. Or the softness in Seth's eyes as he'd seated her next to him. In some districts, dinner partners were seated across from each other. She didn't know which was worse—feeling the heat of his body so close to hers, or having to avoid his gaze if they'd had nowhere to look but at each other.

She'd read Phoebe's letter twenty times since Julie had forced her to hear it, and was no closer to figuring out what she should do than that first night. Had Phoebe meant that Seth was coming back to her, Beth, specifically? That he'd realized his true feelings? Or simply that he'd changed his mind about the trip and gone home, where she happened to be? Oh, how she hated things that weren't clear!

Talk to him, you big silly.

In front of the entire *Gmay*?

Half the Gmay have gone home. Talk to him. This is your chance.

But what if I've read it all wrong and he didn't come home for me?

But this time her panicked mind had no answer for her.

In the *Eck*, Reuben and Naomi Miller had joined the bridal couple on one side, sitting in the place usually occupied by the bride's parents at supper. On Luke's side, since he had no family, Willard and Hezekiah filled that place—he had been boarding with them since his return to the valley. All six bowed their heads and the big room fell silent as everyone said grace.

When the supper helpers brought out the food—all the *roascht* that had been left over from lunch, plus heaping platters of cold beef slices, bowls of horseradish, and steaming casseroles of creamed corn and buttered carrots—Beth realized that in all the racket, it might be safe enough to get this over with.

Seth offered her the bowl of *roascht*, a dish she adored. A second helping today was an excellent thing, in her book. "My favorite," she blurted, then remembered to thank him as she scooped out a portion.

"Mine, too. Too bad we only get this at weddings."

He sounded so normal. So like the man she'd talked with about everything and nothing for hundreds of miles.

"We'll be getting lots of it this winter," she offered. "Including with your sister, next week."

"How much of a sensation will it cause if I ask Susanna to pair us up again?"

Oh, my. Oh, my goodness. From the emphasis in his tone, he'd asked his mother to pair them up now. "You ... would ask her?"

"For sure and certain. Mamm suggested it the day I got home. I've been worried she'd forget—so it was a relief when Gid called your name. Imagine if I'd got Sharon Keim and you got Peter."

Beth was stricken silent. There had been a time when he'd *wanted* Sharon Keim.

"Then I'd have had to make a deal with him to let me sit with you," he went on easily. "I hear Josiah is thinking of taking him on as a hand."

"I heard that, too," she managed. But she couldn't let this precious opportunity to talk to him wander off on trails about other people. "Seth—I have to tell you—I got a letter from Phoebe Plank."

He glanced at her in surprise. "I didn't think you had enough time to become friends."

"Not that kind of letter. She wanted to clear the air. About you."

Now the surprise was stiffening into shock. Or maybe uneasiness. "Me? What did she say?"

"That you were running away." She didn't have it in her to say *running away from me*. "And that you were done with that, and coming home."

"Well, that was true, at least. What did she think I was running from? Her? Because she'd be right."

It took Beth a second to adjust, a second in which she took refuge in a comforting forkful of *roascht* and gravy.

"Why would you run from her?" she managed. "A girl so beautiful? Who clearly enjoyed your company and wanted more of it?"

"Because she wasn't you," he said simply.

He turned a little on the bench and her hands forgot what they were doing with fork and knife.

"Beth, the truth is that I did run away. From you. Like a coward—like a child who doesn't know what he wants. I've pretty much been doing that all my life, not on the outside, but on the inside. Running. Not holding on to things because I would only lose them. I thought that if I taught myself not to let the losses bother me, I could survive them." He took a steadying breath. "The trouble is, not caring about things didn't give me any practice for starting to care about you."

She made a sound halfway between a whimper and a gulp. *Starting to care about you.* The words echoed in her head, begging to be savored over and over again.

"I was a *Narr*," he confessed, his voice low. "An idiot. And it gave Phoebe the wrong impression. She thought I cared about *her*."

"I did, too," Beth whispered. "Nothing has ever hurt so much as watching you drive away in that van."

"I'm so sorry I hurt you like that." He put down his fork to take her hand in his warm one. But the tablecloths weren't long enough to hide anybody holding hands, so he merely squeezed it.

But she could feel it still. Oh, yes. The way she could imagine feeling a kiss for hours afterward.

"By the time we got to the state line, I knew I'd made a mistake. And after that, it was just a matter of buses and trains, taking me home to you as fast as they could go. And then I couldn't talk to you, what with the wedding and everything. These last couple of days have been too hard. It was like a foretaste of a future without you." He shook his head while those words, as bleak as they were, filled her soul with the warmth of certainty.

"So your mother paired us up tonight," she said.

"She's a smart woman."

Beth glanced over at the *Eck* to find Rachel Hertzler gazing at them both, a smile like the dawning of the sun curving her lips. She leaned over to murmur something to her husband, whose gaze met Beth's. He had the best grin. Open and honest and delighted.

Well, there was no mistaking *that*. Those two had engineered this opportunity, and it was up to her and Seth to make the most of it.

"When your mother and Luke leave," she said with a sudden sense of urgency, "and after we help with the cleanup, maybe we can talk more."

"You can count on it."

And even though he had to eat the rest of his dinner with his fork in his left hand, he took her own, their fingers entwining in that magical way they had that day in the van.

She no longer cared that they would be teased mercilessly. That Emily and Tim were sitting right behind them and could see they were holding hands.

The only thing that mattered was that Seth wouldn't let go. Not ever again.

IT WAS NEARLY impossible to be alone at a wedding. No matter where Seth looked, there were people—standing in groups and visiting, walking in pairs along the paths in the woods, even strolling along Creekside Lane listening to the rush of the water.

Finally he said to Beth, "*Kumm mit.* The patio up at the house will be empty."

"But your mother's guests—"

"Archery season for deer is closing soon, and the Inn is full of hunters who get up at three in the morning. They'll all be in bed by now."

The chickens had gone to bed, too, leaving the patio that Luke had rebuilt deserted. Unless someone tried really hard, the two of them wouldn't be visible from either the county highway or Creekside Lane. Seth held out a chair for Beth at the little wrought-iron table where Mamm and Susanna sometimes had coffee, and sank into one beside her.

"I had a surprising conversation with Chris Kauffman earlier." He told her about the man's hopes for a buggy shop, and then about his offer.

"Do you think he was serious?" Beth asked, her warm hand nestled in his. "For true?"

"Chris strikes me as the kind of man who doesn't speak without some thought first. And he mentioned it twice. I think he was serious."

"But I thought you loved cowboying."

"I do. And if someone needs an extra hand at roundup or spring turnout, I'm pretty sure Chris would let me go and help —or even pitch in and help himself." He grinned. "We'd have to teach him to ride, though."

"Montana is a learning experience," she said in the tone of someone who has proved that herself.

He took a breath and chivvied the words into line in his mind. "But the thing is, cowboying is a single man's trade. Going where you're needed. Taking the pay that's offered. Staying in whatever living space is provided, whether that's an unheated travel trailer on the bald prairie, or a comfortable bunkhouse at the Circle M. Those are no kind of places to bring a *Fraa*. And as for *Kinner*, well ..." He let her imagination work on that one.

"There's nothing like looking ahead," she said after a moment. Tentatively, as though she wasn't certain this whole discussion had anything to do with her.

"Exactly. I'm looking ahead. That's what scared me all the way into California, Beth. I convinced myself I had nothing to offer you, no life to make for you, so I ran. Convinced myself that I was doing what was best for you—"

"Without even talking with me about it."

"When I was a child, I spoke as a child, I understood as a child, I

thought as a child: but when I became a man, I put away childish things," he quoted. "I stood there in Death Valley and understood the mistake I'd made. I'd been making decisions in fear, not in faith. And by the time we camped that night and Phoebe made it clear she'd welcome a courtship, it was like I'd grown up. Became a new man. I was done with running away, because there was only one person I wanted to run to." He lifted her hand, turned it over, and pressed a kiss into her palm.

"Phoebe?" she said in a small voice, the kind you use when you're just making sure.

He had to laugh. "Aw, now you're just rubbing it in. She stood there asking for a kiss, and all I could think was that the wrong woman was asking."

"The right one would never ask."

Wasn't that the truth. "The right one doesn't need to," he whispered.

With one finger, he lifted her chin. Her lips parted as if she were about to say something, but her eyes in the last of the daylight said it all. Her lashes fell, and her arms wound around his neck, slowly, as though memorizing every muscle, every tendon by touch. And when he lowered his lips to hers, he discovered that with the right woman, a kiss can make a forever kind of promise, even when she can't find the words.

THE END

AFTERWORD

I hope you've enjoyed the eleventh book about the Miller family on the Circle M Ranch and at the Wild Rose Amish Inn. If you subscribe to my newsletter, you'll hear about new releases in the series, my research in Montana, and snippets about quilting and writing and chickens—my favorite subjects!

I hope you'll join me here: https://www.subscribepage.com/shelley-adina.

Haven't read the first book in the Amish Cowboys of Montana series? Pick up *The Amish Cowboy* on my store at www.moonshellbooks.com. And while you're there, be sure to browse my other Amish novels set in beautiful Whinburg Township, PA, beginning with *The Wounded Heart*.

Following is a glossary of the Pennsylvania Dutch words used in this book. But first, here's a sneak peek at *Rose's July Surprise,* the seventh book in the Amish Romance Birthdays series, where Beth's mother Rose Stolzfus and Willard Zook find love the biggest surprise of all!

Rose's July Surprise © 2026 Adina Senft

She vows never to marry again. He's a confirmed bachelor. But life is full of surprises...

Rose Stolzfus is content with the life she's created in Mountain Home, Montana. Her three children are grown, her rented house is comfortable, and she loves running her own business, Rose Garden Quilts. After a difficult marriage, the widow has all she needs—finally—and has no intention of marrying again.

At fifty-two, bachelor Willard Zook is a lonely man who has just had his heart broken again. By the time he's hired to do some work on Rose's house, he and she have built sturdy fences around their hearts. But before long, it's hard to resist just a peek over the top...

Rose is turning forty-five soon. What will it take for Willard to prove to her that love might be the perfect birthday surprise?

For more, find *Rose's July Surprise* exclusively on Amazon!

GLOSSARY

Spelling and definitions from Eugene S. Stine, *Pennsylvania German Dictionary* (Birdboro, PA: Pennsylvania German Society, 1996).

Words used:

Aendi: auntie

Bischt du okay? Are you okay?

Boppli(n): baby, babies

Bruder: brother

Daadi: grandfather

Dat: Dad

Denki, denkes: thank you, thanks

Dochder(e): daughter, daughters

Englisch: not-Amish people, English language

Englischer: English person

dei: your (lit. thy)

der Herr: the Lord

Fraa: wife

Gmay: congregation, church body
Gott: God
Gott in Himmel: God in heaven
Gottes Hand: God's hand
Gottes wille: God's will
Grischtdaag: Christmas
Grossmammi: great-grandmother
Guder mariye: Good morning
Guder nacht: Good night
Guder owed: Good afternoon/evening
gut: good
Haus: house
hochmut: proud
ja: yes
Kaffee: coffee
Kapp: women's prayer covering
Kind, Kinner: child, children
Kumm mit: come along (lit. come with)
Liebe: love
Lieber Gott in Himmel: dear God in Heaven
Liebling: little love
Liewi: dear
Maedsche(r): girl, girls
Mamm: Mom
Mammi: Grandma
mei: my
Middaag: midday
Middaagessen: lunch
Narr: idiot
narrisch: foolish
neh: no
Nix? From *nichts,* Is it not?

Onkel: uncle
Sohn: son
verhuddelt: confused, mixed up
wunderbaar: wonderful
Youngie: young people

ALSO BY ADINA SENFT

Amish Cowboys of Montana

The Amish Cowboy's Christmas prequel novella

The Amish Cowboy

The Amish Cowboy's Baby

The Amish Cowboy's Bride

The Amish Cowboy's Letter

The Amish Cowboy's Makeover

The Amish Cowboy's Home

The Amish Cowboy's Refuge

The Amish Cowboy's Mistake

The Amish Cowboy's Little Matchmakers

The Amish Cowboy's Wedding Quilt

The Amish Cowboy's Journey

Rose's July Surprise (book 7, Amish Romance Birthdays multi-author series)

The Whinburg Township Amish

The Wounded Heart

The Hidden Life

The Tempted Soul

Herb of Grace

Keys of Heaven

Balm of Gilead

The Longest Road

The Highest Mountain

The Sweetest Song

The Heart's Return (novella)

❧

Breaking Faith

Grounds to Believe

Pocketful of Pearls

Sounds in the Night

Over Her Head

❧

Glory Prep (faith-based young adult)

Glory Prep

The Fruit of My Lipstick

Be Strong and Curvaceous

Who Made You a Princess?

Tidings of Great Boys

The Chic Shall Inherit the Earth

ABOUT THE AUTHOR

USA Today bestselling author Adina Senft grew up in a plain house church, where she was often asked by outsiders if she was Amish (the answer was no). She holds a PhD in Creative Writing from Lancaster University in the UK. Adina was the winner of RWA's RITA Award for Best Inspirational Novel in 2005 for *Grounds to Believe*, a finalist for that award in 2006 for *Pocketful of Pearls*, and was a Christy Award finalist in 2009 for *The Fruit of My Lipstick*. She appeared in the 2016 documentary film *Love Between the Covers*, is a popular speaker and convention panelist, and has been a guest on many podcasts, including Worldshapers and Realm of Books.

She writes steampunk adventure and mystery as Shelley Adina; and as Charlotte Henry, writes classic Regency romance. When she's not writing, Adina is usually quilting, sewing historical costumes, or enjoying the garden with her flock of rescued chickens.

Adina loves to talk with readers about books, quilting, and chickens!
www.moonshellbooks.com

facebook.com/adinasenft

pinterest.com/shelleyadina

bookbub.com/authors/adina-senft

instagram.com/shelleyadinasenft

bsky.app/profile/shelleyadinasenft.bsky.social

www.ingramcontent.com/pod-product-compliance
Lightning Source LLC
Chambersburg PA
CBHW032232050726
47591CB00001B/360